Which Witch?

A Novel

by

Amy Barkman

About "Which Witch?"

"This book was amazing. I could not put it down. I think many kids can relate to Danny being bullied, making new friends, entering God's world, and being insecure about how we look. The characters in the book remind me of myself and some of my classmates. I want to read the sequels! I think grades 6-12 would like it." ~ Dylan G., age 13, grade 8, Kentucky.

"I wouldn't change this book because I like it the way it is. I want to read the sequels. I think grades 3-9 would like it." ~ Heather L., age 13, grade 8, Alabama.

"I wouldn't change anything in the book. It's great and I'm not just saying that to be nice. :-). I learned how to fight bad thoughts. The flow of the book was written very well. I think 4th-7th graders would like it." ~ Katie B., age 12, grade 7, Kentucky.

"This book taught me a lot about Jesus and God and their love for me. I'm glad I have them in my life. I learned about how to win people to Jesus and to fight bad thoughts. I think kids in grades 6-9 would like this book." ~ Kyle H., age 11, grade 6, Kentucky.

"All the kids could be kids I know. I think it's a great book. It's a blessing to have a great Christian book for teens. I learned that to win people to Jesus we should be an example and don't lie. I think kids in middle school and high school would like this book." ~ William R., age 10, grade 5, Kentucky *(author's note: William liked the book so much, he talked his teacher into letting him give a book report on it.)*

"I wouldn't change anything in the book. They won people to Jesus the way I would have done it. I learned to ignore bad thoughts. I think grades 5-6 would like this book." ~ Whitney R., age 10, grade 5, South Carolina

"I don't think it's too scary or too Christian. I really L-O-V-E *Which Witch?* Thanks for letting me read it." ~ Hannah B., age 9, grade 4, Kentucky.

Dedication

This book is dedicated to the children of all ages who have a hunger for the things of the Spirit.

It's dedicated to 7-year-old Marilyn whose parents thought she was crazy when she had an encounter with God. It's dedicated to 10-year-old Stephen who wanted to be a preacher until he found out preachers had to hold funerals. It's dedicated to 16-year-old Patti who longed to be a nun.

This book is dedicated to the Body of Christ and the Lord Jesus who purchased us. This book is dedicated to Jesus' last prayer before He went out to die for us, "that all of them may be one, Father, just as you are in me and I am in you. May they also be in us so that the world may believe that You have sent me." John 17:21 NIV

It is the desire of our Lord that we be one, not that we compromise our doctrines but that we rise above them and unite on the main thing: Jesus is the son of God who came and died for the sins of us all and rose again to give us new life.

He's alive!

Amy Barkman

CONTENTS

Chapter One

New School - Yuck?

Danny almost got all the soap washed off his hands before he was pushed away from the sink. He stood waiting for another sink while the big guy snickered and he washed his own hands. "That's what I like to see … a kid who knows who's in charge. What's your name, kid?"

Danny swallowed to wet his dry mouth. "D … Danny. Danny Alcorn."

"Well, Danny Alcorn. You're new and you need to learn right now that Leo Bailey is in charge around this school. New kids have to pass the tests and your first test is that your dessert is mine today. Get it?"

Danny nodded. *Why was he such a wimp? Why couldn't he be more like the guys in charge? He'd hoped the move and new school would be a fresh start but nothing changed. Because he was still Danny Alcorn, no matter where he was.*

He joined the line in the hallway and when everybody was out of the restrooms, Ms. Gray led the march to lunch. Danny was the first in line and smelled the yummy scent of fried chicken before he saw it, cheese potatoes, and green beans there at the serving table ... Danny's favorite meal, except for the green beans of course. He didn't like anything green but if he had to eat something good for him, they were better than slimy old spinach or broccoli, yuck. Then he spotted his mom placing the dishes of dessert out at the end of the line. His stomach tightened as he saw the chocolate meringue pie. Mom must have asked for this meal for his first day of school. She was always doing something like that to make him happy. Then he remembered Leo. He'd never let Mom know that he had to give up his favorite dessert.

He chose a table in a far corner, hoping the bully wouldn't see him. The only person he'd actually met was there too. Maggie somebody sat beside him in the classroom. He was on the first seat of the first row of desks because Ms. Gray sat her students in alphabetical order. Maggie was at the first desk of the second row. She smiled at him when he first came into the classroom that morning. She told him her name and asked if he'd just moved to town. Nice girl. Nicer than any of the girls in the city school.

She smiled again when he sat down at the table. Several other kids joined them.

"Hey, guys, this is Danny Alcorn. He just moved here from Lexington." She pointed at the others as she called their names. "David, Gretchen, Ray."

Danny nodded but didn't say anything. He was surprised at how friendly the group was to him. Where he came from the races didn't mix much but Gretchen looked like she came from China or Japan or someplace like that, and Ray had skin the color of hot chocolate.

The others talked all through the meal about people and things that Danny didn't know so he just ate in silence. Just as he was about to take the first bite of pie, a hand encircled his wrist.

"Thanks, kid. Glad you don't like chocolate pie." But before the bully could take the dessert, David stood up and looked Leo in the eye.

"You must have misunderstood. Chocolate pie is Danny's

favorite."

How could the other boy have known that? Danny stared at his empty plate, well – empty except for the green beans. Out of the corner of his eye, he could see another boy walk up beside Leo. Then Ray stood up beside David. Ray was very muscular and looked strong. There was a long silence, which was finally broken by Maggie.

"Get over it, Leo," she said. "Nobody invited you. Or you either, Eddie."

Leo didn't answer her but he let go of Danny's wrist and put his hand on Danny's shoulder, squeezing so hard that tears came up in Danny's eyes. "See ya later, kid. Don't forget."

Danny took a bite of chocolate pie but it didn't taste as good as usual.

≈≈

As soon as they returned to the classroom, Ms. Gray announced they would begin the geography lesson. Danny hated geography. Who cared what products were sold by some unknown South American country? Or how many pounds of potatoes came from Idaho?

Just as he pulled out the geography textbook, Ms. Gray said, "You won't need your books today. We're going to play a game." Whoa! That was different. Danny replaced the book in his bag and sat up a little straighter.

The teacher asked for volunteers. Danny didn't catch the name of the first volunteer but David was the second. A girl named Angela with dark curly hair was third.

"We need another girl volunteer." Ms. Gray looked out expectantly over the rows of desks. Danny couldn't see most of the classroom without turning around but there must not have been any more volunteers. The teacher walked past his desk and spoke to the girl just behind him. "Gretchen Andrews?"

It was the other girl from the lunch table. Uh oh. Alcorn, Andrews, how far back could Bailey be?

Ms. Gray was handing out sheets of paper to the four

volunteers when Danny was hit in the back with something sharp. He turned around and saw Leo grinning at him from behind the empty desk. "Don't forget," he mouthed. Danny picked up the ballpoint pen from the floor and put it on Gretchen's desk.

The game was that each of the four volunteers was given the name of a country and would answer questions from the other kids with yes or no until the country was guessed.

Maggie leaned across the aisle, "Kind of like Twenty Questions." Danny nodded but since he'd never played Twenty Questions, he didn't really understand. Just then, Ms. Gray said, "This is a version of the game Twenty Questions. Each volunteer has a list of facts about a country and can answer either yes or no to your questions. If at the end of twenty questions, no student has guessed the country, they will read a fact." She smiled and her eyes kind of twinkled. "The difference is that we're going to rotate between the four, so you will need to take notes. I suggest writing down each of their names at the top of your paper and then listing the facts you learn as the game progresses."

Danny got out paper and a pen and heard Leo retrieving his own pen from Gretchen's desk.

Ray guessed the first two countries, which were Poland and France. A boy named Harold who sat in the fourth row guessed the third, which was Canada. Nobody guessed the fourth one, David's, and the more wrong guesses there were, the more David smiled and at the end when he was giving out hints he laughed a couple of times. Danny saw that Ms. Gray was smiling also.

Wait! He knew it. Or thought he did. What if he was wrong? What if he made a fool of himself? If he got it right, the class would think he was smart. Or would they be mad because he got it and they didn't? While he was trying to decide whether to risk it, Ms. Gray said, "Tell them, David."

"The United States of America!" David announced the answer with triumph in his voice. Ms. Gray laughed. "There's a lesson in itself. Everybody was so busy thinking of foreign places that no one thought of home."

Danny did. But he'd been too chicken to say it out loud. He gritted his teeth.

After the four volunteers returned to their desks, Ms. Gray said it was time for a study period and since it was the first day, they could look over their textbooks or read something else if they had a novel or magazine with them.

Danny pulled out the science textbook and opened it. He was only on the second page when words came to his mind. Three words, "Go To Sleep." It wasn't like he thought the words but like they came to his mind from somewhere else. Right after the words came, a feeling of drowsiness fell on his mind and his eyes. It seemed that the best thing in the world to do would be to put his head down on his desk and go to sleep.

But this was his first day at school and there were kids here who were nice to him. He'd already shown himself to be a coward and he refused to go to sleep in front of the whole class! As soon as he made that decision, the sleepy feeling left.

Danny glanced around the classroom. Most of the kids had their heads down on their desks. Gretchen, Maggie, Ray, and David were the exceptions. He saw them exchange glances, then Maggie looked at him. Just as quickly, she looked away.

Something unusual was going on in Ms. Gray's classroom.

For the first time since he could remember, Danny was interested … at school!

Chapter Two

Double Yuck

Danny ate his dessert every day at lunch, thanks to the presence of his new friends at the table, but his money and the candy he always kept in his pocket were gone by the end of the first week. He'd found out the bathroom was not a safe place. The second week he quit taking anything with him. *I may be dumb but I'm not that dumb!*

Every day during study period the words "Go to sleep" came to his mind, followed by an uncomfortable desire to close his eyes and put his head down on the desk. He always fought the desire, mostly because he noticed that his lunch friends didn't fall asleep even though almost everyone else in the class did. He called Maggie, David, Ray, and Gretchen his friends but really they mostly talked to each other. Maggie and David each tried to include him by asking questions but he just gave him the answer and went back to eating. So they went back to talking to the group and sometimes forgot he was there … or at least it seemed that way.

He was pretty sure they forgot his presence one day when they mentioned 'the club' and also said something about 'spells.'

Danny had heard kids in his old school talk about books on witches so he figured his lunch friends formed a fan club. Since he'd never read the books, or any books for that matter, he didn't pay much attention.

But that afternoon when the 'Go to sleep' words came, he sat up straight before the drowsiness could affect his eyes or mind.

What if my friends are the ones casting a spell over the class? It made sense; they and he were almost the only kids that didn't fall asleep. He noticed that even Ms. Gray yawned a lot during study period, and once even put her head down on the teacher desk. Maybe it wasn't a fan club they belonged to. Could it be a club to practice witchcraft?

He'd rather it be Leo Bailey casting the spell, if that's what it was. *Of course that's what it is, Stupid!* Maggie and the others seemed so nice that Danny didn't like the thought of them trying to control other people's minds.

≋≋≋

Danny didn't take any money or candy to school the second and third weeks but by the fourth week, he felt safe. He'd asked to be excused during second period and was just drying his hands when Leo, Eddie, and a boy called Smelly from the grade behind them came into the restroom.

"Hand it over," Leo said, glaring at Danny as he spoke.

"What?" Danny glared back. His mom worked hard for the money she gave him as an allowance. She meant it for him, not for some bully.

"You've got money in your pocket. Give it to me!"

"No!"

Leo moved behind him before Danny realized what was happening. The bully grabbed his arms and held them behind his back. Smelly sat on his feet and Eddie began emptying his pockets.

When they had all the money, they let him go.

"That should be enough for ol' Dirty Drake," said Eddie as they walked through the doorway and into the hall.

"Shut up," said Leo, looking back at Danny.

Danny took a deep breath, glad they were gone for more than one reason. Now he knew why they called the younger guy Smelly.

But how could Leo have known he'd begun carrying his allowance again? They wanted the money to buy stuff from the custodian! He'd overheard some of the guys talking about buying cigarettes and some kind of books or something from Mr. Drake. It wasn't the first time he'd heard the man called 'Dirty' Drake.

≈≈≈

That afternoon when the words came "Go to sleep" Danny felt the drowsiness immediately and it just seemed too tempting to resist. His eyes got heavier and heavier, and his head went down to be cushioned by his arms on the desk top.

He wasn't sure how long he'd slept when Gretchen woke him, shaking his shoulder. There was drool on his arm. He turned around and nodded, and mouthed the words, "Thank you." As he glanced over the classroom, everyone was asleep but his four lunch partners.

Then he saw Gretchen and Maggie giving each other what he'd come to think of as *the look*. Hmm.

≈≈≈

That night Danny had a hard time falling asleep. He'd always stayed alone when his mother worked night shift. 'Course it was different now since she was driving back to Lexington and wasn't even in the same town. It hadn't bothered him the last month, so why was he afraid tonight?

It seemed like he could almost see the dark shape of a man over in the corner right past the window. But when he turned on the light, there was nothing there. Danny left the lamp on and after a lot of pillow thumping and turning over in bed, he finally fell asleep.

It was a green place, not green the color of grass and trees but a sick green, the color of infection and vomit. He was trapped in the green and didn't know how he got there or how to get out.

There was no definite shape to the green, just forms that kept changing. He thought part of the green was a chair, only to see it suddenly look like a tree. When the green looked like a chair, he felt tired and wanted to sit, but when it became a tree, he wanted to climb. As soon as he wanted to climb, the green looked like a bathtub. He tried looking away at other parts of the green but the other parts were also changing shapes that made him want something, only to change when he started to get it. There was no one else around and he realized with a sickening feeling that he himself had no solid shape either. He wasn't green but he was shapeless like the green. He wanted to scream but he had no mouth and no voice.

After what seemed like a long time of the horror of being a shapeless mass in the middle of shapeless masses he began to see a change. There was a yellowish light forming behind some of the green shapes, filling the green background with itself. The yellowish light began to take form, and the form looked like that of a man. Danny thought briefly of the dark shape he thought he saw in the corner before he turned on the light in his room but he dismissed the thought – that was a dark shape and this was light.

It was scary to be thinking in a dream of something that happened when he was awake, and to know he was dreaming.

The light form shimmered brightly and gathered itself together in a brilliant burst of green–shattering splendor and before him stood a man. With relief, Danny saw that he also had a human shape again. He would have been embarrassed to have no shape in the presence of the man.

The man laughed, "Don't worry, my son. I will always help you find your real self. I will never leave you."

No man had ever called Danny "my son" and though the presence of the man was a little scary, Danny liked the way the man made him feel – like he belonged.

The man held out his arms and said, "Come to me. Come to me of your own free will and you will be mine forever and you will never again feel alone and I will let no one bully you. I will be your father forever and you will be my son."

Oh, the relief of it – the joy of having a father of his own, someone to protect him! Danny wanted to run into those open arms more than anything he had ever wanted to do in his life, but something stopped him. The something seemed to come from inside and kept his feet from moving, and at the same time he heard a voice calling his name urgently. He knew the voice didn't want him to run into the man's arms.

"Danny! Danny!" He thought the voice was Maggie's, or maybe Gretchen's. But then …

"Danny! Danny! Wake up!" It was Mom.

She was sitting on the side of the bed, shaking his arm. He was embarrassed when he realized that his cheeks were wet and he had been crying.

"What's wrong, son?" Mom looked worried. "It's not like you to fall asleep with the light on." She very kindly ignored the tears but felt his forehead for fever. "Your temperature feels normal."

"I'm okay," he said. "Just a nightmare." But he really didn't feel okay.

"I have good news," she said happily. "I was going to tell you in the morning but I saw your light and … well, I'm glad to tell you now. I have a new night job here and don't have to go back to the city anymore. I got the letter in the mail today and opened it when I got in. The job is just for supper and I should be home by eight every night. Isn't that great?"

He smiled. "Yes, that is really great."

"It won't be quite as much money as I was making before at my night job – in fact it won't be nearly as much but the school job pays better than I was making in my old day job and they'll about balance out. Besides, the rent here is cheaper."

"I am really glad, Mom," Danny said. He meant it.

Chapter Three

Surprises

Danny couldn't stop thinking about his dream last night. It was scary but he remembered how much he'd wanted to run into the man's arms. Something about it didn't seem right.

"Danny!" Ms. Gray was standing over his desk. "Did you hear the question I asked you?" He hadn't.

"I know! I know!" The guy named Harold over in the fourth row was waving his arms. Ms. Gray looked at Danny once more and then sighed. "All right, Harold, you may give the answer."

Here I go again looking stupid. But maybe he wouldn't have known the answer after all, even if he'd heard the question.

At lunch, Danny decided he was going to bring up the "Go to sleep" thing. The group never talked about it, at least not where he could hear, but surely they noticed everybody else falling asleep. Maybe they caused it. But would Gretchen have woken him up if she was part of making him fall asleep?

"Can I ask a question?" Danny spoke quickly as soon as the last of the four sat down at the lunch table. All eyes turned to him.

Maggie smiled. "Sure, what?"

"This command, or whatever it is, that makes everybody go to sleep in study period. Are you all doing it?"

Maggie's lips quit smiling and got very tight as her eyes narrowed. "Of course not! Why would you think that?"

David made a motion to Maggie. "We're not mad that you asked, Danny. But what makes you think it was us?"

"Well, you are the only ones who never go to sleep, except me. And I know I'm not doing it."

Ray laughed. "We thought you were casting the spell until yesterday when you fell asleep."

Gretchen nodded.

Maggie shrugged. "Well, yeah, I guess I can see why you thought that. It's just that we …" David reached over and touched her arm and she closed her lips tightly.

Danny went on. Might as well tell them all his thoughts. "I'd heard you talk about some club and also about spells and stuff so I thought maybe you were reading those witch books and had a club to learn how to do spells on people."

David touched Maggie's arm again as she opened her mouth like she was going to speak. "No. It's not us," he said.

≋

Right before study period that afternoon, Ms. Gray asked Danny if he would run an errand for her. He stood up and followed her out in the hall. She held out a slip of paper.

"I want you to take this down to the basement to Mr. Drake's room. He's the school custodian. Do you know where it is? The sign says 'Supplies.'"

"Yes, Ma'am." Danny saw the room every day on his way to and from gym class. He also saw some of the guys go into Mr. Drake's room at times.

"We need him to do a more thorough job cleaning our classroom." She shook her head in disgust as she handed him the paper. "Thank you, Danny." She returned to the class.

Danny went down the two flights of steps to the basement and knocked on the door of the supply room. There was no answer. He slowly opened the door and looked in. There was an old battered desk off to the right with a corkboard above it covered with notes stuck with thumbtacks and so dirty that it looked like it must have all been there back when Ms. Gray was a student. The desk was covered with empty cans of Pepsi and candy wrappers and half eaten packages of chips. There were crumbs all over the place and the floor was much filthier than Ms. Gray's classroom.

"She should see this!" Danny thought out loud. "She'd be glad about our room." He decided to lay the note down on the center of the desk because he knew if he put it on the board, it would never get noticed. Then he thought maybe the note wouldn't get noticed on the desk either and maybe he should take a thumbtack and put it on the door. He knew he shouldn't pry into other people's things but he had a perfectly good reason and so he opened a drawer of the desk to see if he could find a thumbtack. He saw no thumbtack but he saw something else.

It was a bottle of whiskey.

Danny knew that nobody, not even grown–ups, and not even school staff, was allowed to have whiskey on school grounds. He closed the drawer quickly.

He went back out into the hallway and closed the door behind him.

Then he did what he knew he should have done in the first place when no one answered his knock. He slid the paper underneath the door.

What now? He wished he hadn't seen the whiskey but since he did, what should he do about it?

The noise from the gym interrupted his thoughts. Coach Adams. He was everybody's favorite teacher. Even Danny liked him although gym class was not a happy time for him. He could tell Coach Adams about the bottle and let him do whatever he thought was best. Or could he?

≈≈≈

In gym class, the boys were playing basketball while the girls and Ms. Gray watched from the bleachers. This made Maggie furious and everybody knew it.

"It … it's sexist!" she pouted as she complained to the group.

Even Danny knew by now that she liked Coach Adams very much, but didn't like him to separate the boys and girls during team sports. Others pointed out that the girls got to practice during the second half of the class while the boys sat on the bleachers, but it didn't help her mood. She reminded them that they weren't even playing yet, just learning how to handle a basketball "the Adams way."

Danny was really trying, for the first time in his life, to learn to dribble a basketball and run at the same time. It wasn't easy even though Ray made it look like something any three year old could do.

Danny was concentrating on dribbling when Leo kicked his own basketball directly at Danny. The basketball hit Danny in the nose, which immediately started to bleed. Coach Adams blew his whistle and everybody got very quiet. Ms. Gray came down from the bleachers but Coach Adams got there first and gave him a towel. He told Danny to stay sitting upright, and lean forward just a little.

Danny did what the Coach said and then Coach Adams walked toward the other end of the gymnasium where Leo Bailey and Eddie Jackson stood with smirks on their faces.

Danny was surprised to see Harold Sands come toward him looking worried. The other boy had paid no attention to Danny since school began. Why would he suddenly look worried because Danny got hurt?

Harold bent down and said in a low voice, "She made him do it. I saw her …"

But just then a basketball came flying across the floor just as viciously as the one that hit Danny in the nose. This one hit Harold in the side of his head and he fell over. Danny knelt beside him but Harold didn't open his eyes.

Nobody knew where the second basketball came from. Nobody saw it until Harold fell.

Harold wasn't unconscious long but when he came to, he couldn't remember anything that happened since gym class began.

Danny was sure that the whole thing had been caused by whoever the "she" was that had "made" Leo kick the ball at him.

Was it the same person who gave the command in study period? Was it Ms. Gray?

≋

"It was nice of Coach Adams to bring you to the kitchen when you got hurt today." Mom had rented a movie like she always did on her night off. They settled in front of the television with butter-flavored popcorn and colas.

Danny nodded. "He's everybody's favorite teacher."

When the movie was over, Mom turned to him with a serious look on her face.

"Do you know anything about books with kids who are witches or books on how to cast spells?"

"I've heard about 'em but never read 'em."

"Good," she said. "I've been wanting to talk to you about things like that."

Danny was surprised. Mom never talked about anything much except money, work, and movies and, sometimes, family things about when she was a girl and lived at home with Gramma and Grampa.

Danny saw his grandparents only once a year, at Christmas time. They always sent plane tickets for Mom and Danny to fly out and spend a whole week in the country on a real farm. Those were the times that didn't seem like real life – special times, outside of the real world of going to school and being home alone with the doors locked so no one could hurt him. The week at Christmas and Mom's nights off were the … well, if life was a sentence, those times would be like parentheses – a break in the sentence. *Good grief! I'm taking school way too seriously these days!*

"You want to talk to me about the books?" He forced his mind back to the subject Mom brought up. "But I haven't read 'em."

"No." She patted the couch beside her. "Come here and sit beside me." He moved from the chair to the middle cushion of the couch. "I want to talk to you about God."

Danny was even more surprised.

"Ever since we moved, it's like I can think more clearly. In the city it seems like the air itself is filled with busyness and I never had time to … to really think about things. It's been a good thing for me to walk to and from work, especially in the mornings before there is anybody on the streets."

Danny didn't know what to say so he just nodded. He kind of liked walking to school and back himself. Since he went later, there were people on the streets but he was feeling better these days than he could ever remember. He just hadn't thought about it much until Mom brought up the walking part.

"I need to ask you to forgive me." She looked at him as she put her arm around his shoulder and hugged him.

"Mom!" He squirmed under her hug. If she had done something bad, he didn't want to hear it.

"You see, I was baptized when I was about your age. I am a Christian. I know you know about Jesus and God but I have never taken you to church or taught you like I should have. I guess …" She stopped and he could see her swallow hard. "I guess when your dad left I just gave up on anything good happening in life and I was just so tired trying to make a living for us. I quit going to church and just sort of forgot about God. Well, there is really no excuse but now, since we have moved, I want things to change."

Danny was even more surprised. He knew that every year Gramma and Grampa talked about Jesus and he knew they went to church all the time. He and Mom went with them on Christmas Eve, but his mother had never acted interested and so he thought it was just something old farm people believed in and did, not anything that had to do with him and Mom or here and now.

"You are going to start going to church?"

"*We* are going to church," she said firmly.

Chapter Four

Church?

"I was brought up in the Methodist Church but if you have friends who go to another kind of church, where you could join a good youth group, we'll try that." Mom smiled at him. "You decide."

Danny didn't know what to do. The only people he could call friends were the four who ate lunch with him. Though Mom had not gone on to mention any more about witches, he got the impression that church and witches didn't go together. They said they weren't the ones causing their classmates to become sleepy after lunch every afternoon but they did talk about witches. So he didn't want to bring up church. The group might stop having lunch with him.

Every day the rest of that week before she left for her night job in the city, Mom asked Danny if he had asked his friends about church yet. Every day Danny said, "No."

Mom didn't push it, but Saturday morning she woke Danny up

and told him they were going to the store to get him a new outfit. They had just gotten new clothes before school started and that wasn't even two months ago, she said this outfit was to go to church in.

Danny was surprised when they had to get a size smaller for him. He'd noticed his clothes were a little looser and figured it was because of not eating candy during school and also the walking, but he didn't realize he had lost that much fat. He looked in the mirror at himself and thought maybe he wasn't as ugly as he used to be.

The next morning they got dressed up—more dressed up than they ever had been, because even when they went to Gramma and Grampa's church on Christmas Eve nobody ever got dressed up. Mom really looked pretty and for the first time Danny wondered why she didn't date. He heard other kids in the school in the city talk about their Moms dating when they were divorced.

Danny didn't like the tie that Mom tied around his neck but she said he had to wear it for church.

"I thought we'd go to the Methodist Church," said Mom. "It's just a block past the school. Do you want to drive or walk?"

Danny thought a minute. "Walk," he said. All of a sudden he realized that it wouldn't embarrass him or make him feel like a baby to be seen walking with his mother to church.

When they got there, the organ was playing and a man met them at the door and handed them each a folded paper with a picture of the church on the front and the list of what was going to happen printed inside. And the inside was pretty inside. Every time Danny had ever been to church, it had been night and he had never seen how the light came through the colored glass windows and made colors in the room, almost like being in a rainbow.

He looked at the paper and was glad to see that there were stars by the places where they were supposed to stand up. He would hate for his mom and him to do something wrong their first time there.

Three people walked onto the platform and a group in robes

came in and sat at some benches over to the side facing the rest of the church. Danny didn't see anybody he had ever seen before. A man prayed, that was one of the times they stood up, and then some more people came onto the platform – two of them had guitars. Mom whispered to Danny, "Back when I went to church, nobody ever played guitars."

A movie screen came down from the ceiling and words came on it and the people up front began singing and everyone   in the church joined them. They sang happy songs; songs about God making the day special and how much He loved them and how He gave His son to die so they could go to heaven and how He wanted them to be happy now. Danny didn't know the songs but he liked them and he felt like maybe some day, after he had heard them enough, he might try to sing along with them.

When they sat down again, a woman got up and made some announcements about things that were going on in the church … one was called a Halloween Alternative Party. Some other stuff happened that was boring and they took up money. Then he got a surprise. On the program was listed, right before the "Message," the "Bell Choir." A group of young people came up to the front and he noticed that the long tables in front of the platform weren't tables but great big xylophones.

What really surprised him was that two of the kids were Maggie and Angela from his class and some others he recognized from the lunchroom. He had seen Angela reading the wizard kid books in the library and he knew that Maggie was in a club that talked about witches and spells, so he was surprised that they were at church. It was very confusing.

Danny thought the message was boring. The man talked a lot about sports, which Danny was not interested in, and he also said that people should give more money to the church, which Danny thought was selfish. But his mom seemed to be happy and that was what was important.

≋

Back in school, Maggie and Angela didn't mention seeing him

at church, so Danny didn't say anything either at first. Of course he and Angela had never spoken. Angela was a pretty girl, probably the prettiest girl in the whole school and even if Danny had been the kind of boy who talked to girls, he wouldn't have the nerve to talk to Angela – she was too pretty and too smart. He never saw her talking to anyone else either. She was always reading a book.

Finally, after a few days, he couldn't stand it anymore. He hadn't planned to say it, but the words just flew out of his mouth as soon as Maggie and Gretchen sat down beside him at lunch. "I saw you at church Sunday. I liked the bells."

Maggie smiled. "I saw you too. I didn't know you were Methodist."

Danny was a little embarrassed. "Well, I'm not really. My mom is. We didn't go to church in the city, only when we went to visit my grandparents." He hoped that Maggie wouldn't ask how often he went to his grandparents and find out he only went to church once a year.

"I'm glad you're coming now. Are you coming to the Halloween Alternative Party?"

"Oh yeah, I heard about that. What is it?"

"It's a really fun thing for Christians to do instead of celebrating Halloween."

Danny had never celebrated Halloween in the city because Mom always had to work but he knew other kids dressed up in scary costumes and went around to places asking for candy. Mom said when she was little they went to homes in the town and it was a lot of fun, but people had gotten mean and some had given poison and dangerous things to kids and now parents just took their children to shopping malls and the businesses gave out candy.

Maggie continued, "We dress up like Bible characters and have pizza and play games. Why don't you come?"

By then the boys had joined them and David said, "Yeah, we all go to Maggie's church for the party even though we go to other churches with our families. Her church has a lot of fun stuff for kids to do."

Danny turned to David. "Where do you go to church?"

David said, "Word of Life Church – it's new, it's not a denomination, just Christians."

Ray said, "I go to 1st Baptist but, like David said, I go to Maggie's church for a lot of stuff too."

Danny looked at Gretchen who laughed. "I'm Presbyterian. Harold Sands goes to my church too." But her lip curled slightly and Danny could tell she wasn't happy about it.

David proudly said, "Coach Adams goes to my church!"

Coach Adams was awesome. He made you do the work in gym class but he never made fun of you or embarrassed you like Danny had seen some other coaches do. Danny suddenly wanted to go to Word of Life Church. He decided he would tell his mother that night.

≋

"No. I don't approve of those new kinds of churches that don't have anybody to account to. That's the kind of place that turns into a cult and all kinds of bad things can happen. We'll stick to the Methodist Church."

She said, yes, he could go to the party on Saturday night.

Danny had never dressed up in a costume in his life and he didn't know any Bible stories except about Adam and about Jesus.

"I won't go naked except for a fig leaf, or dressed like a baby dragging a manger behind me!"

Mom laughed. "I promise we'll think of something."

Chapter Five

Haunted House

For a boy who was never interested in anything except food and television, Danny found his world turned upside down. He liked math and history, he enjoyed playing volleyball in gym class, and he wanted to know more about God ... and witches.

He decided to read the books that everybody liked so much – the stories, not the spells. Since he had to put his name on a long waiting list in the library, it would be a while. He felt a little uncomfortable about it since his mom had said she was glad that he hadn't read them. But if the librarian at school approved ...

That day at lunch he asked the others what they were going to dress as for the party at the Methodist Church.

Maggie spoke up first. "David will be David again as usual. What is it this year, giant killer or King?"

David laughed. "This year of all years, can't you guess?"

The others exchanged knowing looks and said in unison, "Giant Killer!"

They all laughed. Danny didn't get the joke but he smiled.

Gretchen said, almost too quickly it seemed to Danny, "I am going as Queen Esther."

"Ruth for me," added Maggie.

"Moses," said Ray. "My dad made me some … well, you'll have to wait and see. I am going to win the prize this year!"

"Oh yeah?" said David.

"Yeah," said Ray with great assurance.

"Who are you going as?" Maggie asked Danny.

"Well," he said shyly. "I thought I might dress up as Daniel. Nothing big, just a bathrobe and a stuffed lion I had when I was a little kid."

"Good idea," she said. "I'm glad you're coming."

After school that afternoon, he was starting down the steps to walk home when Leo, Bugger, and Smelly blocked his path.

"You coming to the Haunted House tomorrow night?" Leo asked.

"What haunted house?"

"The one my dad's lodge puts on every year. It's real scary. You too chicken to go?"

"I'm not chicken!" said Danny.

"Then we'll see you there."

Danny had noticed a paper on the front bulletin board at the school about a haunted house but he hadn't paid much attention to it. He had never been to a haunted house before. He didn't like Leo and didn't think he would like his father either but a haunted house might be a fun thing to do.

As he walked on, he saw Angela Wicker looking at him and shaking her head.

Suddenly he felt bold.

"What?" he asked.

"You're going to do all that baby stuff? Haunted houses, anti–Halloween parties?"

"The party is at your church," he protested.

"It's baby stuff," she said. She walked on.

Mom was going to be working her last weekend in the city but she agreed that he could go to the haunted house on Friday night as well as the church party on Saturday. Both were within walking distance of the apartment. She told him that when she was a girl there were haunted houses in her community and they were fun and just a little scary.

"They decorate with fake spiders and the people have you feel peeled grapes and tell you it's eyeballs, and they hand you spaghetti and macaroni and tell you they're intestines. Usually somebody's father sits up in a dimly lit coffin when you walk by."

≈≈≈

Friday night it was already dark when Danny let himself out of the apartment and walked to the lodge that was on the other side of the street two blocks away.

Just like Mom had said, there were fake cobwebs and spiders at the entrance. He paid the three dollars and was led by someone dressed up like a mummy into a dimly lit small room draped with scarves. The mummy left him there. Either the scarves were all green or the light was green and making them appear to be green. A small fan was blowing the scarves and suddenly Danny began to feel afraid.

The scene reminded him of his dream of the green that kept changing shapes. Just as he was thinking about following the mummy back through the doorway, a woman draped in black came in the room. He couldn't see her face because it was covered with a veil, but she was dressed exactly like the witch in the movie Snow White.

The witch sat down at a small table that was also draped with green scarves, or with scarves turned green by the light. She pulled out a crystal ball from somewhere in the huge draperies of black that she wore and set it on the table. She began cackling – a witch cackle that almost, but not quite, seemed so fake that it wasn't scary.

"I see ..." she began. "I see ..." she repeated. She stopped. Danny thought he heard her breathe in sharply as though she was surprised. He looked at the crystal ball, then breathed in sharply himself. For the crystal ball was filled with green shapes changing slowly like a mono–colored lava lamp. The green was not the color of grass and trees but the color of infection and vomit.

Danny felt something rise in his throat and he wanted to run out but his feet seemed glued to the floor. He stared at the ball and saw a yellow light begin to disperse the green and then the ball was filled with blackness and all the lights in the room went out.

≈≈≈

When Danny got back to the apartment, his hand holding the key shook so much he could hardly open the door. He didn't care what Leo would think if he found out Danny hadn't finished going through the haunted house. He just wanted to be home, but now that he was home, he was still afraid.

He wished Mom already worked at her new job. He wished it was tomorrow night and he was at the church party dressed like Daniel who was not afraid of anything, standing beside David who could kill giants.

Danny put both latches on the door and turned on the television. A blood–curdling scream led him to discover that every channel was filled with horror movies in honor of the season. He turned it off.

Just then, the phone rang and Danny eagerly ran to get it.

"Danny, is that you?" It was Gramma.

"Yes, Gramma. Mom's at work."

"I know. She called and told me about the new job and said tomorrow night is her last night in the city. I am so glad for you both."

He waited. His grandmother had never called just to talk to him.

"Danny?"

"Yes, Gramma?"

"I know it's unusual – me calling like this. But I was worried about you. Are you okay?"

"I am fine, Gramma," he lied.

"Are you sure?"

What could he say? That he had a nightmare and then got scared at a haunted house? It was too silly.

"I'm sure."

There was a long pause.

"Okay, but do you mind me praying for you?"

He knew Gramma prayed for him all the time. Why was she asking all of a sudden?

"No, I don't mind."

She meant now. "Father, I hold up Danny to you and I thank you that he belongs to you through the covenant of baptism. I thank you that the blood of Jesus covers him and protects him from all danger, spiritual and physical. Watch over him and keep him safe. In Jesus' Name I pray. Amen."

They were both quiet for a few seconds and then Danny said awkwardly, "Thank you."

After she hung up, Danny wondered what she had meant by him belonging to God through the covenant of baptism. When his mom got baptized, did that somehow do something to him? He didn't understand any of it. But somehow the call had helped and he wasn't so afraid any more. He picked out a video and settled down to watch.

≈≈≈

On Saturday, Danny and his mom got his costume together. He guessed it was because she was so interested in the costume party that she didn't quiz him much about the haunted house. When she asked he just said it was like when she was a kid, fake spiders and all. He was relieved that the subject was not brought up again.

It was almost time for her to go to work when he remembered about the phone call.

"Gramma called last night," he said.

His mom looked surprised. "I told her I was going to be working."

"She called to pray for me."

"Well! What was that all about?"

"I don't know but she said something about me belonging to God through the … the c … the something about baptism. What did she mean?"

Mom smiled. "She meant that you were baptized when you were a baby. Oh! Look at the time … I'll be late. Of course it's my last night. What can they do? Fire me?" She laughed as she hurried out the door.

Baptized! Did that mean he was a Christian? Did that mean he really was a Methodist like Maggie?

Suddenly Danny heard the command, "Go to sleep." It shocked him. He was used to hearing it at school and almost enjoyed refusing to obey it, but the words had never come to him in his home. It scared him. It was like having an animal that was fun to watch behind bars in a zoo suddenly show up in your living room. It scared him and it confused him. Suddenly the drowsiness was too strong to fight and he laid down on the couch.

He was back in the green, the sickening, disgusting green. Only this time the shapes moved more violently than before. This time they were not looking like chairs or trees or bathtubs but like spiders and mummies and witches. He tried to scream but again he had no mouth and no voice. He needed to breathe but he had no nose. There was no air, only the green that smothered him. Then, just as he had given up and was ready to die, the yellow light started to filter into the green. Then the green was gone and the man was there. This time he said nothing but held out his arms. Danny wanted to run into them for protection but suddenly he noticed that the man's lips were bright red, like a vampire.

Chapter Six

The Party

This time, the phone woke him.

"Hello," he answered breathlessly.

It was Maggie. "I got your number from the operator since you're not in the phone book yet. I didn't know if you remembered that the price to get into the party is a can of food for poor people."

"No ... no, I didn't know that. I hadn't thought about it, it being at the church and all."

She laughed. "I know. They'd let you in anyway but I thought you might rather have one."

"Yeah," Danny said. "I would. Thanks for calling."

After they hung up, he looked at the clock. Six thirty and it was already dark outside. Mom left for work at five, so he had been asleep for over an hour. He shuddered. He was glad that he had something to do tonight. He was glad that it was in the church. He just wished that he didn't have to walk through the dark streets to get there.

The party was fun. There was lots of pizza for everybody. Danny had forgotten how much he liked pizza. He and Mom didn't have it very often because it wasn't in their budget. He especially liked sausage pizza and there were lots of sausage pizzas on the large table along with pepperoni and plain cheese and vegetable pizzas.

True to her word, Angela Wicker was not at the party but Danny thought she was crazy. It wasn't a baby party at all. There were grown–ups, and kids of all ages. The adults played the games too. To his own surprise, Danny won a prize for drawing the funniest face on a gourd. The prize was a giant bag of M&M's with two movie coupons attached. He grinned. *Now I can take Mom to the movie since she won't be working late at night.* Life was finally starting to feel good.

During the costume parade – when he and Maggie had already taken their turn and were watching some of the others being judged – he said, like it wasn't really important, "I guess I am a Methodist. I was baptized when I was a baby."

She turned to him with sparkling eyes. "I knew it! I just knew it!"

He frowned. "What do you mean?"

She looked confused. "Oh, I can't really explain. It would sound silly to you I think. But I just knew that you … well, that you belong to the King."

The term "belong to" made him feel strange.

"What do you mean, belong to?" He could hear the hostility in his own voice and wished he could take the words back but it was too late.

She looked away from him and back at the judging. "I told you it would sound silly. Just forget it." They sat there in silence.

Ray's dad had made two rounded top concrete tablets and wrote words that looked like Hebrew on them before the concrete hardened. There was a small amount of explosive powder in the indentations where the words were written and when "Moses" lit the fuse at the back, the "Hand of God" caused the words to be lit up and seen by all. The entire party burst into applause and Danny knew even before the prizes were announced that Ray was right when he said he'd win.

The group of five that always sat together at lunch walked out together. Danny summoned up some courage that he hadn't known was there.

"I want to thank you guys for having lunch with me every day. It really helped me ... since I'm new and all," he finished lamely.

Maggie shot a triumphant glance at the others.

David said, "You're welcome." Danny knew he was right; it was a decision the group reached together. He didn't understand why they decided to include him but he was glad because their friendliness gave him even more boldness. He really didn't want the evening to end and have to walk home alone in the dark.

"Can I ask you guys something?"

"Sure," said David.

"Are you all learning spells and stuff? You know, witchcraft and wizardry and all that?"

"Certainly not!" said Maggie indignantly.

Danny felt his face turn red. "I'm sorry. It's just one day I heard you say something about spells and a club ..." The four faces froze. He stammered on. "I just ... I mean ... I thought ... I thought maybe you had formed a fan club – the books and all."

"Have you read the books?" asked Ray.

"No, but I'm on the waiting list," Danny answered honestly.

"Don't read them!" said Maggie.

"Maggie!" David admonished. "You can't tell Danny what to do or not do." He looked at Danny. "We decided not to read them. They may be fun to read but we think they open up minds to stuff the Bible warns against."

"Oh." Danny wondered even more about the club, but they didn't seem to want to talk about it so he didn't bring it up again.

Just then, Maggie's parents came out and offered them all a ride home, so Danny didn't have to walk in the dark after all.

≋

The next morning he and Mom went to church again and this time Danny sang along with some of the music. He saw his mother smile at him and he could tell she was pleased. He still would rather go to the church that David and Coach Adams went to but he didn't say so.

Yesterday afternoon's nightmare seemed far away in the presence of the music and the rainbow light of the church. But he remembered it and made up his mind to ask David about the command.

The preacher wasn't so boring today. He talked about Jesus more and how he healed the sick. He said that God still heals the sick, only now He does it through doctors. That made sense to Danny since Jesus was gone to heaven. Danny was glad to find out he had been baptized as a baby. It made him feel like he belonged to the church.

He thought of Maggie saying he belonged to the King, whoever that was. He remembered how angry he'd sounded when he answered her. He didn't like the idea of belonging to a person … except a father of course. That would be different. The man in the dream was like a father. Could that have been the King Maggie was talking about? In the first dream, he seemed really wonderful, but Danny remembered the red lips in the second dream and shuddered.

He looked in the bulletin – now he knew that was what the programs were called– and saw that there were some classes starting for young people. They were called Confirmation Classes. Something inside of him got very excited.

That afternoon Mom called the pastor on the telephone and made an appointment for them both to talk to him after school and before she began her new night job on Monday.

≈≈≈

Danny managed to get David off alone after lunch Monday.

"What about this "Go To Sleep" thing that happens in Ms. Gray's class?"

David nodded, "We wondered when you would bring it up. We noticed you don't let it get to you …"

"Except that one time when Gretchen woke me up."

"Right. What do you want to know?

"Who's giving the command?"

David shook his head. "We don't know."

"It happened to me at home on Saturday."

David looked horrified. "What?"

Danny nodded. "Yes, and I didn't fight it and I had a nightmare. A nightmare I had before, the night after I fell asleep in class that day. The first time my mom woke me up and then on Saturday Maggie called and woke me up."

"At home. That's bad." David shook his head. The bell rang for them to return to class. "Listen, Danny, we need to talk. What are you doing after school?"

Danny's face fell. "Usually nothing but today my mom and I are going to see the Methodist preacher."

David nodded. "That's good. But I'd like you to … well, I'll have to talk to the others."

After school, Danny and his mom visited Reverend Baxter and arranged for Danny to take the Confirmation class that was going to meet at Sunday School time before church. They decided that the day the class was confirmed, Mom was going to join the church too.

The next day at lunch the group was more quiet than usual and Danny could tell there was a strain. He wondered if it had anything to do with him. He felt like Maggie and David wanted to let him in on their club secrets but Ray and Gretchen didn't want to. He wasn't sure why he thought this, but he did.

That afternoon before school ended, a thought occurred to him. He had seen the four of them go off together many afternoons. Maybe they were going to this mysterious "club" of theirs. He decided that today, if they went off together, he would follow them.

≈≈≈

It was a deserted chicken coop and looked like something out of an old "Our Gang" movie. The screen didn't filter out any of the sound and, hidden behind the hedge, Danny could hear every word.

Maggie sounded very sure of herself. "I KNOW the King wants him in the club."

David said, "But Gretchen may be right. He said that he heard the command at home – and he gave into it."

Ray spoke next. "We just can't take a chance on opening the door to the other side."

"Danny is NOT on the other side!" Maggie practically shouted.

Ray was calm. "I didn't say he was on the other side. Obviously the other side has gotten a place in his mind. Until it is gone, until we are sure that he really belongs to the King completely, we can't take a chance. The other side wants him bad."

"Badly," said Maggie and sighed heavily.

Then Danny heard a voice he hadn't heard before begin talking about something else. From what he could tell, it sounded like the group were telling problems about their families and classrooms and stuff, and then they all prayed about them.

That didn't seem like much of a secret club to Danny.

Chapter Seven

The Clubhouse

Danny was unhappy again. There was a strain on the conversations at lunch and now he knew for sure that it was because the group disagreed about him. That made him feel bad and he also felt bad because he had spied on his friends and found out their secret, even if it didn't seem much of a secret.

He felt more left out than he ever felt in his life. Because never before had he almost been "in."

But the group kept sitting with him at lunch and he was grateful because he knew they kept Leo and his friends from bullying him during lunch.

Every afternoon in study period, he continued to fight the command "Go to sleep." He decided to play detective and discover who was giving it. If he did that, maybe the others would trust him.

After a week, he had a list of those who didn't always fall asleep. The list included himself, Maggie, Gretchen, David, Ray, Angela, and seven other kids. It had to be one of those who were giving the command. He first eliminated the six of them, including himself, because they were "church people." He would have said Christian but the term made him uncomfortable. He felt like there was something more to being a Christian than he himself had, but he knew that there was something special going on with him. He figured it was church.

Wait, that wouldn't work. Harold Sands was a "church person" and he still fell asleep every afternoon.

Danny was thinking over these facts one day during study period when he remembered something that caused him to sit upright so abruptly that Maggie looked over at him with curiosity.

He remembered the day he got hit by the basketball and wondered, "What if it's Ms. Gray herself giving the command?"

≈≈≈

"It makes sense," said Maggie.

Danny caught up with her that afternoon leaving school and asked if they could talk. They were now slowly walking along the sidewalk toward his apartment building. Maggie lived several blocks beyond so she walked the same route Danny did, although she was usually walking with a group of girls – unless she had a "club" meeting.

"This is the first year it's ever happened," she went on, "and it's the first year we've had Ms. Gray."

Suddenly Maggie stopped. "Are you in a hurry to get home?"

"No," he shrugged. "Mom's gone into work already."

"Come on." She turned and headed back toward the school. "I want to take you someplace."

He had a sick feeling that he knew what that someplace was, and when she turned off onto another street before they got to the school, he was sure of it. Maggie was going against the decision of the group and taking him to their secret clubhouse.

Danny got more miserable the farther they walked. Maggie trusted him enough to go against the others. But he knew he couldn't be trusted. He'd sneaked and pretended, and he felt awful. Finally, when they were almost to the deserted lot where the chicken coop stood, he couldn't stand it any longer.

"Wait!" he stopped.

Maggie turned around and looked at him impatiently. "What's wrong? We're almost there."

"I know," he said sadly.

"What do you mean, you know? You've never been ..." But she stopped. The look on his face was a full confession. "You followed us?"

Danny nodded.

"Well! Of all the sneaky ..." Maggie stopped and was quiet a moment as if she was thinking hard, or listening.

Then she smiled. "It's okay. The King wanted you here. The others were just too stubbor ..." She stopped again. "The others just can't see it yet – that you are one of us."

She started walking again. "C'mon."

The lot was grown up with hedges, bushes, and tall grass. If it had been in the city, somebody would have made the owners mow the grass, trim the brush, and tear down the chicken coop. But they were in a small town and the place was perfect just like it was.

Other than the chicken coop, the only thing standing was a fireplace made out of fieldstone. Danny thought there was probably a family who warmed their hands there a long time ago. The "club" had cleared a path that couldn't be seen from the street so they could enter and exit without getting covered with burrs or having their clothes torn by thorns.

"I hope you don't get in trouble for bringing me here." He added loyally, "I won't tell, I promise."

Maggie grinned. "I will." She laughed at his startled look. "I can't keep it a secret. That's one of the rules. We can't keep secrets."

That made him feel better. He'd tried not to think about it but he had felt a little, no – to be perfectly honest he'd felt a lot, betrayed by David. He took the information Danny shared with him and used it to side with the ones who were against Danny being brought into the club. If it was a club rule that you couldn't keep secrets then it didn't feel so much that David was a traitor.

As before, the "clubhouse" looked just like what it was – a chicken coop. Before they went inside he helped Maggie prop up the wooden windows that covered the screen "so we can breathe" she said. When they entered, Danny was surprised. The group had really worked on the inside and with the sun shining in, it looked like a real clubhouse should look.

The walls were painted a light blue and where the chickens used to roost were books and art supplies all wrapped in clear plastic to keep rain from coming through the wooden slat windows and ruining them. There were pillows scattered on the floor, each also covered with some kind of plastic protection. Some were covered with black garbage bags and some with white garbage bags, some with clear zippered bags like blankets come in, and some double bagged with plastic grocery sacks.

"There's more than just you four?" Danny asked, even though he already knew the answer, not just because of the pillows but because of the strange voice he heard the day he spied on them.

"Yes. We are the only ones out of our class at school – and we are the ones who started the club." Danny could hear the pride in her voice. "There are seven of us all together. You'll make eight."

Danny frowned. "But what if the others don't vote me in?"

She laughed. "It's not that kind of a club. We can't vote. The King brings people in."

"But you brought me," he protested.

She laughed again and shook her head.

She unwrapped a pillow that had "Maggie" embroidered in wobbly letters across the surface and then turned thoughtfully to the other wrapped seats.

"Scooter won't mind. You can use his seat." She unwrapped another pillow with the same kind of wobbly letters.

They sat down on the floor with the plastic coverings carefully placed under the pillows to keep them from getting dirty, and Maggie said, "Okay, now. We just be quiet and wait for the King."

"Huh?"

"You'll see. Just close your eyes," she commanded.

For a moment, his old fear that his friends were behind "the command" surfaced, but he refused to think that, and did as she said.

For a long time they sat in silence.

Then Maggie began talking. In a few minutes, Danny realized that she was praying but it didn't seem like praying at the time – it just seemed like talking.

"King Jesus. We know you are here because you promised that when any two of us come together to meet with you, you'll be with us. Help us to hear you and see you. Danny and I need you to show us what to do."

They sat for a long time again in silence. Danny started to get uncomfortable. Scooter's pillow was not very thick and the dirt floor was starting to feel hard.

He had a sudden vivid memory of the man in his dream and a bolt of fear shot through his abdomen. Was this the King? Was the man with the red mouth Jesus? As much as he'd wanted to run to the man for protection in the first dream, the feeling was that strong that he wanted to run from that man now, here, in this place. If that man was Jesus, then Danny didn't want Jesus. He knew it without a doubt.

What was going on?

Then, suddenly, without warning, Danny felt warmth on his shoulders. At first, he almost opened his eyes to see who was there but something stopped him. It was like a blanket was carefully placed around him, only the blanket wasn't made of wool or cotton. The blanket was made of love. Without reasoning, somewhere deep inside, he knew the difference between the false Jesus and the real Jesus.

Danny didn't ever want to move from this place. He hoped Maggie wouldn't say anything. He didn't want the silent love to ever stop. He just wanted to sit there in it forever.

He was aware in his mind of a light, a light with a shape like a man, but still just light. Words began coming to his mind, and they were almost the same words that the man in the green dream had spoken but there was a big difference in the way they made him feel. The words were, "I love you. I will be a father to you and you will be a son to me. I will make my home in your heart and I will never leave you or forsake you." The words came from the light but it wasn't a yellow light, it was a white light, a clean clear light – and the light loved him.

Then the words and the light were gone and he was aware again of Maggie and the clubhouse.

He wasn't sure how long the light and the words had been there. Later when he tried to talk about it, it seemed like it had only lasted a second. At the same time, he felt like he had always been in the presence of that light and those words – it seemed that the light and the words and the love were his true home and he had just found them again.

He was loved.

Life would never be the same.

Chapter Eight

Danny's First Meeting

Danny was so excited that he could hardly go to sleep that night. Maggie unwrapped one of the book bundles before they left the Clubhouse and gave him a paperback New Testament in an easy to read version.

For the first time in his life, Danny Alcorn was eager to read!

Mom noticed his light still on around eleven p.m. and knocked on his door.

"Are you okay, son?"

"Yes." Then he added proudly, "I'm reading the Bible."

There was a long silence outside the door. Then she said, "I guess those confirmation classes are working."

He said, "I guess so."

But he wondered. He laid the Bible down and thought about it. Were the classes working? They seemed boring to Danny – a lot of history, only without battles or interesting stuff. He decided that Confirmation Class didn't have anything to do with what was going on with him and his new relationship with Jesus.

The Bible slid to the floor and the place where Danny had been reading was lost. When he picked the Bible up, it fell open to a place further back and Danny read …

"We know that God makes all things work together for the good of those who love Him and are chosen to be a part of His plan." This was in the book of Romans, the eighth chapter, verse 28. "Hmmm." Danny thought about it. He got the message. Mom taking him to church and the Confirmation Class and the group at lunch and Maggie believing in him – all those things worked together to call him to Jesus. He went on reading.

"God knew from the beginning who would put their trust in Him. So He chose them and made them to be like His Son. Christ was first and all those who belong to God are his brothers." That was verse 29. Danny laid the book down again. That was too big a thought for him to understand. He, Danny Alcorn, was chosen and made to be like Jesus? Jesus was the firstborn of many brothers? He had always heard Jesus called God's "only begotten son." What did this mean?

He fell asleep thinking about these new thoughts, with the Bible face down on his stomach and the light on.

≈≈≈

Danny could tell as soon as he entered class the next morning that Maggie already told the others about taking him to the Clubhouse. David shook his hand, Ray grinned, and Gretchen touched him on the arm, each one making wordless gestures of acceptance. He was glad that there was a meeting that afternoon because he had about a million questions.

Danny could hardly wait for school to end that day. It was almost like the old days at school in the city. Only back then he wanted school to end so he could go home and watch TV and eat candy. Now he wanted school to end so that he could go to the Clubhouse for the first time to a real meeting as a real member.

≈≈≈

The club was called The Fun To Be One Club and it was called that because even though they all went to different churches, they were all Christians. One day shortly after they had found the chicken coop and decided to meet together there,

Kyleigh had looked around at the others and said with heartfelt satisfaction, "It's fun to be one!"

Kyleigh was a red–haired, green–eyed, soft–spoken girl who was a year younger than the members in Danny's class. She and Scooter, whose pillow he had sat on the day before, were in the same room at school. The other member of the club was Polly who was a year ahead of his class. Polly was an American Indian. Her last name was Talltree and she went to the First Christian church.

Danny asked his first question. "Since all the churches are Christian churches, how come only yours calls itself the Christian church?"

Polly shrugged. "I don't know. I think it's because they wanted to be just Christians and not a denomination – not set themselves as separate from the rest of the Christians." She paused. "But it didn't work. It became another denomination."

David nodded. "That's kind of like my church. It started to try to be non-denominational and just follow Jesus but then it and the others like it became like a denomination even though they are not really connected together. They changed and started calling themselves inter-denominational but it's really not. Most of them have really strong beliefs about Christianity and think they are right and everyone else is wrong."

"That's why we are together," said Kyleigh. "We are … what's that word?"

"Trans–de–nom–in–ation–al!" blurted Scooter triumphantly. It was obvious that he had been practicing the word until he had it down pat. "We are transdenominational."

"That's right," said David. "Gretchen thought of the word to describe us."

Gretchen just smiled. Danny had learned that Gretchen never said very much.

Kyleigh added, "We'll probably find out that someone else used it first – just like the Fun To Be One Club."

Danny was surprised. "There are more Fun To Be One

Clubs?"

Kyleigh's eyes sparkled. "At least one. David found it on the internet."

Danny thought she didn't look at all upset that someone had the idea for the name before she did.

David said, "We're trying to figure out how to get our parents to let us go there next summer."

"Go there?"

They all nodded and began talking at the same time. Polly stopped talking and held her hand up in the air. It was the way his first grade teacher had gotten the class to be quiet – hand in the air, mouth closed. The club members did just like the first graders and closed their mouths as they put their hands in the air. Here it didn't seem like a baby first grade thing but grown up, a way to keep order without saying a word.

"Let's let David tell about it," said Polly. "He's the one who found it."

They all looked expectantly at David, even though six of them already knew what he was going to say. "It's a real place," said David. "It started a few years ago with some people wanting to get churches in the same town to work together to help people. They called it the Fun To Be One Club and they had monthly dinners for people, and programs, and they formed a drama team …"

"And a dance team!" added Maggie.

"… and a dance team," said David. Polly nudged Maggie who was sitting beside her.

"They started doing stuff at fairs and festivals and they had a radio program in their local area," David continued. "Then somebody gave them a lot of money and they built a Clubhouse."

"A big Clubhouse," said Scooter, who was then nudged by Ray.

"It is big, a retreat center really. People go there and stay for weekends or for weeks. They have regular camps in the summertime and it sounds great!"

Maggie held up her hand, just like in class asking permission from the teacher to say something.

David grinned. "Yes, Maggie?"

"Can I show him the book?" David nodded and Maggie went over to one of the book bundles and extracted a large flat book that reminded Danny of a fairy tale book that his mother used to read him. It had pretty pictures in it and was still in his room at home.

"It's called Kingdom Tales," said Maggie. "It says that they are from the library at the Fun To Be One Club Clubhouse. Now that you are a member, you can come here and read it whenever you want. Just be sure and put it back in the plastic."

"You think your parents will let you go there?" Danny wasn't at all interested in the book. He had just gotten interested in reading the Bible and he didn't want to waste time on some silly fairy tale book.

"I think so," said David. "Coach Adams approves and he will talk my parents into it."

"Coach Adams knows about the Fun To Be One Club?" asked Danny.

David nodded. "Yes, Polly and I thought we needed an adult, kind of like a sponsor, like other clubs. He doesn't come to the meetings but he knows about them and we go to him if we have any problems. Any one of us can go to him."

"Like if we have a problem ourselves, or if we think that one of the others is, well, getting off track or something," Polly added.

Danny didn't say anything but since he knew that his mother didn't trust the church that Coach Adams and David attended, he didn't think that she would trust the Coach's choice of summer camps. Then he brightened up. Maggie's parents were Methodists. Maybe if Maggie's parents agreed to let Maggie go, she would agree, and she didn't have to know about Coach Adams having anything to do with it.

Then he realized that even if she agreed that it was an okay place, summer camp was not in their budget.

Chapter Nine

Thanksgiving

The next day, Tuesday, was the last day of school before a five-day Thanksgiving break, and Danny was not happy about that. He grinned at his own frustration. Whoever would have believed that Danny Alcorn would be sorry that school was out? But he was. He would miss his friends. There couldn't even be any Fun To Be One Club Meetings during the holidays because Maggie, David, Kyleigh, and Scooter were all going away with their families and Polly, Ray and Gretchen were all having family come to visit.

The only good thing about it was that he could go to the Clubhouse all by himself and maybe, just maybe, he might have another experience with God. He didn't know exactly what to call the Person he had met that day in the Clubhouse with Maggie. It wasn't exactly Jesus the way Danny knew him now but it seemed like it was partly Him. It seemed like partly the Father, the one that Danny thought of as God Himself. Whoever it was, Danny wanted to be with Him again.

≈≈≈

Danny fell in gym that Monday and even though it was just a

twist of his ankle, not a sprain or break or anything, Coach Adams took him to his mother in the kitchen again.

He heard her talking to Gramma that night and saying something about "a good role model for Danny." That sounded good for the future and the Fun To Be One Club! He was glad that he hadn't told her the Coach went to Words of Life Church.

The Coach invited Danny and his mom to help at a Thanksgiving Day meal that the community churches were having for poor people in the high school gymnasium. Since they didn't have any family around, it would be a special thing for them to do on the holiday. They would get to eat, too.

Danny found himself more interested in different kinds of food lately. He always complained about turkey dinner in the past but now he thought maybe he might like it. He was beginning to wonder if he had really not liked some of the food his mom used to try to get him to eat or if he just complained about it to be … well, just to be stubborn. He found out that he really liked the green beans they cooked in the lunchroom. It was the first green thing he had ever liked. Salad was still yuck and brussel sprouts were sickening but green beans were good and peas were … well, he could swallow peas.

≈≈≈

The Fun To Be One Club was meeting right after school Tuesday for the last time before vacation and Danny was eager to tell them about Harold and what he had said before he got hit in the head that time in the gym. He hadn't told them about the bottle in Mr. Drake's drawer and wondered if he should tell them.

If I tell anyone about the bottle, they might think I was snooping. Then he thought again. *Well, weren't you?*

Danny laughed to himself. The way his mind worked these days reminded him of some old fashioned cartoons he had seen on TV where a character would have a devil on one shoulder whispering in one ear and an angel on the other shoulder whispering in the other ear.

He decided to go with the angel every time! So he told the

others about finding the bottle in the drawer and he confessed that he had used the excuse of looking for a thumbtack to snoop. No one said a word about the snooping for which he was grateful. But they all thought he should tell some adult about the bottle.

Maggie and Kyleigh thought he should tell the principal, Mrs. Carpenter. David and all the others thought he should tell Coach Adams, and let the Coach decide what should happen next. That sounded good to Danny, though he would rather not have to confess about the snooping to the Coach. But it hadn't been so hard with the Club and he thought he could do it again.

Then he told them what Harold had said, "She made him do it. I saw her …"

"Scareeeeeeee!" said Kyleigh. "That's real witchcraft!"

"It's real witchcraft to make almost all the kids in a class fall asleep," said Maggie.

"Yeah, and believe me, it works. It happened to me twice. Besides that, it let something in, something bad, because after it happened, I had nightmares and something really bad wanted me to give myself to it." Danny told her earnestly.

He hadn't told anyone the exact details of his dream but he did then.

"I'll bet the bad thing that wanted you has also gotten into some of the others in the class," said Maggie.

"Well, it wasn't controlling Harold when he was trying to warn me."

"But now he can't remember who he saw?" asked David.

"He can't even remember that he saw anything," said Danny sadly.

"I wonder about that ball," said Maggie thoughtfully.

"What do you mean? Which ball?" David questioned.

"The ball that hit Harold. No one saw anyone throw it. Do you suppose she has gotten so good at it, at witchcraft, that she can make a ball move by itself, and not just influence minds?"

The others stared at her with horror.

The meeting ended with prayers for safety for all those who

would be traveling over the holidays and for wisdom to know what to do next to fight the witchcraft that seemed to be growing at Southport School. All the Club had accomplished so far was to keep themselves from obeying the command to "Go To Sleep" and wake up a few people who gave into it. It wasn't enough.

The spells were growing stronger.

≈≈≈

The dinner at the High School was a good thing, Danny decided as he crawled into bed Thanksgiving night. It felt good to be part of helping people who didn't have as much as you did.

It was the first time Danny ever experienced that. He had spent most of his life feeling sorry for himself that their budget didn't include a lot of fast food or computers or trips to Disney World. But this afternoon he saw some really poor people, some of them lived in cars, and some of them didn't have cars to live in but slept in boxes or under bridges. Some of the people who didn't have a place to live were families with children. Seeing them made Danny feel truly thankful for the first time ever on a Thanksgiving Day.

But he didn't want to be like the guy in the Bible who was thankful that he wasn't like other men, so he wasn't sure how he should feel about it. Being a Christian was wonderful, but it could be confusing sometimes.

Danny had worked very hard at the dinner. He set up all the chairs and carried salt and pepper shakers to the tables beforehand. Then he carried bowls and platters to the tables during the dinner, helped dry dishes, and folded all the chairs back up when everyone was gone. By the time they got home, he was exhausted and decided he could wait until tomorrow to read his Bible; after all there was no school. He turned off the light.

"Go To Sleep." The words came to his mind clearly.

He sat up in bed and turned the light on. "Go away, you! Get out of my mind. Jesus is the only one allowed in my mind. Go away!"

And it did.

Danny picked up the Bible and turned to Romans 8. He never stopped being amazed at the words there – *"So He chose them and made them to be like His Son."* The thought was still too big for him, but he believed it. God wanted him, Danny Alcorn, to be like Jesus.

Chapter Ten

The Controlled Mouse

"She's been practicing," said Gretchen, her black eyes narrowing.

The eight of them were seated on their pillows in the Clubhouse. Polly had brought Danny a pillowcase with familiar wobbly letters embroidering his name that she made during the Thanksgiving holiday. That meant his membership was really official!

David just shook his head. "Wasn't it unbelievable today?"

The other four students of Ms. Gray's class nodded in agreement.

"What happened?" asked Polly. "You have all been hinting and rolling your eyes all the way here. So tell!"

Maggie started to say something, then closed her mouth and looked at David. He grinned. "Go ahead Maggie. It started with you."

"It ended with me too!" she said disgustedly. She turned to Polly. "The first thing that happened was that my book fell off the desk. I don't know how it happened; I didn't touch it. It just fell off the desk onto the floor. Ms. Gray gave me one of those disgusted looks but I hadn't done anything … it had been in the center of my desk! I leaned down to get a pencil out of my bag when all of a sudden I heard it hit the floor. I couldn't believe it."

"Maybe you accidentally moved it when you bent down." Polly suggested.

Maggie shook her head with determination. "No way."

She continued. "Then the next thing that happened was the first mouse …"

"No," Danny interrupted. "The next thing was the map."

Maggie nodded. "You're right. We were in history class when Ms. Gray pulled down the map. Later when she was turned away from it, not touching it with the pointer, all of a sudden it flew back up into the metal tube.

"That happens all the time," said practical Polly.

"Not when it has stayed down perfectly still for five minutes," responded Maggie impatiently.

David intervened. "We knew, Polly. We all just knew, even before we talked to each other. Somebody caused it."

"We're pretty sure that it isn't Ms. Gray because she wouldn't do that to herself. She was surprised when it happened," said Gretchen.

Ray added, "And I KNOW she didn't cause the mice!"

Kyleigh and Scooter were not saying a word during the discussion but sat listening with wide eyes.

Polly was quiet but her mouth was all tight like she thought they were reading more than was there into some perfectly ordinary things.

David prompted Maggie, "Then the mice."

Maggie nodded, "Yes, the mice. Yuck!" She shuddered before continuing. "The first mouse ran from the back of the room to the front, then turned around and went back. Ms. Gray didn't see it but a lot of the girls screamed."

"And the second mouse?" Kyleigh asked almost in a whisper.

"Ran to me," Maggie said with disgust. "Like the first one, it came from the back of the room, ran up to the desk, circled around, then came straight toward me. It touched my shoe and was going to crawl up my jeans. I just know it. Yuck!"

"What did you do?" Polly was taking them a little more seriously now.

"She drop kicked it!" said Ray. "As good a drop–kick as any football player." He laughed.

David laughed too. "The mouse landed on Ms. Gray's desk and lay there stunned."

"Ms. Gray didn't know what to do," said Danny. "She just stood there looking at the mouse."

"We thought it was dead," said Gretchen.

"But then it got up, ran down the side of the desk, and guess where it went?" Ray asked.

Polly guessed, "Back to Maggie?"

The others nodded.

"Right back," confirmed David.

"What did you do?" asked Scooter.

"I jumped up on my chair and it started climbing the chair."

"She jumped off her chair over on the side near my desk." Danny took up the story. "That old mouse climbed down the other side of the chair and went at her again."

"That mouse was after Maggie!" said Gretchen. "She ran up toward Ms. Gray's desk and it followed her."

"What happened?" the other three asked in unison.

"Smelly," said Maggie.

Polly, Kyleigh, and Scooter looked shocked.

"Smelly?" The younger two asked in unison.

The others nodded and Maggie explained. "Smelly Borden knocked on the door and that mouse stopped dead in its tracks, just stopped, like it was wondering who was at the door. Then Smelly came in and gave a note to Ms. Gray."

Kyleigh and Scooter, who were in Smelly's class, nodded. Scooter said, "Yeah, Miss Sims sent him with a note but I didn't know who it was for."

"Anyway," Maggie continued, "when he came in, it was like

that mouse got set free and it turned around and ran back toward the back of the room as fast as it could."

"Set free?" Polly frowned. "What do you mean?"

David said, "We think that someone was controlling the mouse and making it go after Maggie. When their concentration broke, the mouse was free to leave. And it did!"

Scooter laughed. "Poor mouse."

Maggie glared at him. "Poor mouse! What about me?"

"This is really serious," said Polly, and she turned to Gretchen. "I think you are right. She has been practicing."

Ray added, "What scares me is that I think she is still practicing."

Polly frowned, "What do you mean?"

Ray hesitated a minute, then went on. "Think about it. She caused someone to throw a ball – at Danny – with mind control. Then she caused a ball to hit Harold that no one saw anybody touch."

David nodded. "That could have been by accident."

Danny frowned "That was no accident! He was about to tell me who she was."

David shook his head. "No, what I meant was that when she saw him come to you, she realized that she'd been spotted then maybe she just panicked and caused it to happen without thinking it out. Then she realized that she could cause things to move by themselves."

Ray nodded, "They call it psychokinesis."

"Now she is practicing on our classroom, " said Gretchen, seeing what he meant.

"Yes," said David. "She is getting stronger."

Maggie hit her fists together. "But who is she? I'd like to send a mouse up her blue jeans!"

Danny wanted to laugh but the others looked shocked and Polly said, in a parent kind of voice, "Maggie!"

Maggie didn't look at all repentant but she looked down and muttered, "Well, I would."

David intervened. "What we need to do is ask the King."

Maggie looked up with hope. "Yes. Let's."

They all bowed their heads and closed their eyes. David led the prayer.

"Father, we come to you in Jesus' Name and ask you what to do about all this stuff. You said that if we would ask for wisdom you would give it so we are asking. What can we do to stop this ... this ... these spells from getting stronger and controlling our classroom?"

The eight club members sat in silence for a long time. Danny started getting uncomfortable and could feel the hard dirt floor under his pillow. His mind started wandering. He never made it here alone over the holidays because the weather had turned cold and it was just easier to stay at home. But he had begun to feel like Jesus was really there with him when he read his Bible. At first it had been easier to feel God's presence when he was with the others, now it was easier when he was alone. Again he thought, "Christianity is confusing."

He wondered if the others were feeling God and hearing what He had to say. They were so quiet for so long that he was beginning to feel like maybe he really didn't belong in the club. He hated sitting on the floor for so long in silence. It wasn't so bad when they were talking, but just to sit here?

Just then a verse from his Bible flashed into his mind. He could see it clear as anything; it was on the left hand page about two thirds of the way down the page. *"Stand against the devil and he will run from you."* Danny didn't know what book, chapter, or verse it was but he could see that one verse as clear as if the book were in front of him and his eyes were open. Before he had time to talk himself out of it, he spoke.

"Stand against the devil and he will run from you."

He opened his eyes and looked around to see the reactions of the others. They'd all opened their eyes too. They were looking at him with respect.

"That's it!" said David.

Danny wondered what was it.

"We've been just sitting back protecting ourselves but we need to take a stand against him – oppose him." David said firmly.

"Yeah," said Ray. "Like in football. There is defense and offense. We need to take the offensive."

"How do we do that?" asked Maggie.

"We need to find out who is working the spells," said Gretchen. She grinned. "Then tackle them?" she teased Ray.

"Do we?" Danny asked, then wished he hadn't because all eyes turned to him and the smiles left their faces.

He stammered. "I mean, do we have to know who is working them? Can't we just fight the spells? " Nobody said anything so he went on. "Couldn't we start with the sleep one?"

They were all so quiet that he thought they were thinking he was stupid for suggesting it and didn't know how to tell him.

But then David shook his head and said quietly, "Why haven't we thought of that before?"

Chapter Eleven

Forgiven

The next day they did it. They all prayed during lunch, Polly alone, Scooter and Kyleigh together, and the other five in a group. All eight prayed the same prayer, the one they made up and wrote down.

Dear Lord, we want to be Your Body in our classroom to stop the witchcraft. We don't want to use our minds like witches and wizards do to make things happen our way and just be more powerful than them, but we want You to use us to stop the spells. When the command 'Go To Sleep' comes today, we are going to fight it, not just for ourselves but for the others in the room. We are going to do it in Your name and in Your power and we thank You that You are showing us how. In Jesus' Name, Amen.

They agreed to each pray the prayer out loud sometime during the lunch break, and that during the time of study period, all would be thanking Jesus for being stronger than the spell and for keeping all the students awake.

And they did.

It worked.

As soon as the command came, Danny looked around and

started thanking the Lord that He, Jesus, was bigger than any witchcraft spell. Harold's head was already on his desk and five other students looked asleep too. That was almost victory already – usually there would have been nearly three times that many heads on desks. But one by one each of the six raised up their heads and picked up a book or a pencil. Harold was the last to shake it off but within five minutes, the whole class was awake and studying.

The five Club members gave each other "the look" and it was full of triumph!

≋

After gym period that afternoon, Danny asked Coach Adams if he could talk to him sometime. They decided to meet right after school since the Coach had a few minutes before practice.

Danny was a little nervous. He didn't like to be a tattletale but he knew that some of the things Mr. Drake was doing were really wrong and could hurt the kids. He was also shy about admitting to Coach Adams that he had been snooping through someone else's belongings. But he decided that the sooner it was over, the sooner he would feel better, so he hurried to the gymnasium wing as soon as the dismissal bell rang. The Coach's office was right off the locker rooms, connected to them and the outer hallway.

Coach Adams looked up from his desk and smiled when Danny knocked on the frame of the open door. "Come on in, Danny. Let me just finish this memo so we can talk." He motioned to a chair right beside the desk and Danny sat down.

Danny had never been in the Coach's office before. There were two diploma's framed and on the wall and some other framed picture about children living what they learn. A copy of the Ten Commandments engraved on small stone tablets stood on a file cabinet and over the cabinet was a framed embroidered picture of flowers and Psalm 23. Danny was glad to see those signs of Coach Adams' belief there for anybody to see who walked in the office. It made Danny feel proud to be a part of that belief.

The Coach laid the pen down and turned to Danny. "Now, how can I help you?"

Danny glanced at the open door to the hallway. Coach Adams understood and got up to close the door, then returned to his chair. "This is serious, huh, son?"

It made Danny feel warm inside that the Coach had called him "son." It also made him ashamed to tell about the snooping but he burst out with it.

"I snooped in Mr. Drake's desk." He looked into Coach's eyes expecting to see disgust but instead saw patience as he waited for Danny to explain.

"Miss Grey sent me with a note. He wasn't there and I should have put it under the door but ... well, the other guys call him "dirty Drake" and they buy something from him and I ... well I told myself I was looking for a thumbtack to put the note on the bulletin board but I think I really just wanted to see what was in his desk."

Coach Adams nodded but said nothing.

"Then I ... well, I saw a bottle of whiskey. I knew that was against the rules and I wish I didn't know about it. But now I do, so I asked the others what I should do. Some said go to the principal but most said go to you and you'd tell me. So here I am."

Danny wanted to drop his head, but he didn't. He looked right in the Coach's eyes as if to say, "Now, if you want to tell me how bad I am ... go ahead."

Coach Adams nodded. "Yes, this is serious. I am glad you came to me first."

Danny's heart pounded.

Coach smiled for the first time. "Yes, it was wrong of you to snoop. You've asked God to forgive you?" It was a question, not a statement.

Danny thought about it. He was sorry that he looked in the desk but he couldn't remember asking God to forgive him. "I don't think so, Sir."

Coach held out his hand. "Then let's take care of that right away." He bowed his head and there was silence. Danny realized that the Coach was waiting for him. He slipped his hand into the larger hand and bowed his own head.

"Dear God, please forgive me for snooping in Mr. Drake's class."

There was silence.

And the silence kept on.

"God, please forgive me for wanting to see what the boys are buying from Mr. Drake."

Coach Adam's hand squeezed Danny's before he spoke. "Father, thank you that you are working in Danny to bring him close to you. Thank you that you not only forgive him for the wrong things he did but you clean his heart from the reasons for those wrong actions. Father, I ask now that you do away with any further consequences of those wrong motives and actions in this situation. Lord, thank you for protecting Danny from seeing what he was trying to see. In Jesus' Name, Amen."

Danny sighed, then realized that he had been holding his breath all through Coach's prayer. The two looked at each other and laughed. The Coach's eyes twinkled. "Glad that's over?"

Danny smiled. "Yes, Sir."

Coach Adam got a serious look on his face. "Son, I am going to report this but I don't want your name brought into it."

Danny looked surprised but didn't say anything.

"I can handle this without saying how I got the information."

Danny sighed again, a big deep sigh. "Thank you, Sir."

Coach Adams stood up and put his hand on Danny's shoulder. "You're a good boy, Danny. Stay close to Jesus, and always tell the truth and tell your friends not to talk about what you saw."

Danny nodded. "Thank you, Sir," he said again.

The sounds of basketballs on the gym floor announced that it was time for practice, so Danny left by the hall door while Coach Adams went into the gymnasium.

Danny wondered if any of the other Club members had ever

talked to the Coach about the witchcraft stuff. He thought they should.

≈≈≈

That night Danny watched TV while he waited for his mother to get home from work. There were a lot of advertisements promoting Christmas.

Christmas was just a few weeks away. It was going to be Danny's first Christmas as a Christian. Well, it would be his first Christmas since he asked Jesus to come into his life. He still didn't understand about this baptism thing. Had he been a Christian all along because he was baptized?

He had mixed feelings about the annual trip to his grandparents. It would be good to go back to their little church on Christmas Eve now that he understood about the celebration and was a part of the new life that began when Jesus was born. But he didn't want to miss out on the Christmas celebration with his new friends either. He was glad the choice wasn't up to him.

He found himself thinking about what he could give his mother for Christmas. This was a first! Always before, Danny thought only about what he would get for Christmas. Always before the only thing Danny gave his mother was whatever Gramma wrapped for her under the tree and marked from him; and he never knew what it was until Christmas morning when Mom opened it. This year was different. Christmas seemed to have crawled into his heart and he wanted to give something to his mother from himself. But what? He had no money and he didn't know how to make anything.

While he was thinking about how to get a gift for her, he heard his mom's key in the door. She came in smiling. "There you are! Have you eaten supper yet?"

"No, not really. I ate a sandwich right after school."

"Good!" she said, putting some sacks on the table. "I brought home some leftovers from the diner. Let's eat while it's still hot."

They settled down to country fried steak, mashed potatoes and gravy, peas and yeast rolls. It was wonderful to have Mom working in town and coming home early enough to have supper together.

After they ate, she told him about Christmas.

It turned out that there was no choice for anybody. Just starting a new job meant that Mom couldn't take off for a whole week.

Now that the annual visit wasn't going to happen, even though he knew it didn't make sense, because an hour earlier he was undecided about what he wanted to do, Danny was disappointed.

In just a few moments, it seemed as if his only excitement for the year had been taken away from him and life was very unfair. No plane trip, no home-baked cookies, no winter farm scenes, no Gramma and Grampa.

Danny pouted. "You are spoiling all my fun," he said, in the tone of voice he used to use a lot. He saw the shock in his mother's eyes when he spoke.

He knew he shouldn't act that way, that it would only make his mother feel bad. But he couldn't seem to stop himself. She told him things they could do for fun here in their new home but it didn't make any difference. He still pouted.

Mom looked sad when they said goodnight and went to their own bedrooms.

When Danny said his prayers, God felt far away.

What was wrong? It had been such a good day … the group's success with the command and no children being under its power, being forgiven by God and Coach Adams about his trip to Mr. Drake's room. But now, almost sick inside with disappointment about the holiday trip, feeling mad at Mom for something she had no control over, God felt very far away …

Confirmation was a week away, the third Sunday of Advent, and tonight Danny felt much less like a Christian than he had when he started the confirmation classes. What was wrong with him?

Chapter Twelve

Angels and Devils

The next morning Danny left for school thirty minutes early so he could go by the gymnasium wing. Coach Adams was there in his office working but he immediately put his paperwork aside to talk to Danny.

Since the Club members hadn't talked to the Coach about the witchcraft battle, Danny didn't betray their confidence, but he did tell Coach about his dreams and the haunted house. He also told Coach how he acted last night to his mom.

Coach Adams smiled at him kindly and began his response with the previous night's problem. "Son, every Christian in the world has times like that, times when we just act ornery and then get mad at ourselves! I like your cartoon explanation of the devil on one shoulder and an angel on the other. I think that is pretty accurate concerning truth – except that those warring "words" are in our hearts and minds, not outside ourselves."

Danny smiled back, the first time he had smiled since supper last night. That made a lot of sense. Those "warring words" in his mind and heart.

Coach went on. "You've got a lot of years of self–centered

thoughts planted in your heart and it's going to take a while for God to weed them out and let His Word about who you really are grow up to fullness."

Danny could feel himself relax.

"Now, why were you so surprised at yourself acting that way? You used to act that way all the time from what you say."

Danny was startled. "Well … I'd been, well, I've been acting good." He felt his face get warm. "I mean, I'd been different and I was glad. You know … I was …"

Coach grinned, "Proud of yourself?"

Danny grinned back, sheepishly. "Yeah, I guess so."

"Why have you been proud of yourself?"

"Well, some of the other kids don't care about God and church and stuff." He was quiet, really searching his heart and mind for the answer. "I think I thought I was better than them." He looked at Coach. "But I'm not, am I?"

Coach shook his head with a gentle smile in his eyes. "More blessed, perhaps, not better. What do you think would bring that extra blessing to you?"

Danny thought. "Maybe because people pray for me … my Gramma maybe?"

Coach nodded. "Could be. So what does that tell you?"

"That I should pray for those people?" It came from his mouth as a question.

Coach Adams nodded.

"Whenever you get to thinking that you are really something, remember what Proverbs 16:18 says: *Pride goes before destruction and a haughty spirit before a fall.*"

Danny laughed. "That sounds like what happened to me, all right. I won't ever be prideful again!"

The Coach laughed. "Watch it! That too is a form of pride." Then he got serious again.

"I'll tell you something. There are lots of weaknesses we can overcome and not ever have a problem with again. But pride is one that seems to follow us around our whole lives – all of us."

Danny thought that was a scary thought.

"Do you remember the prayer I prayed for you yesterday, that God would forgive you and also cleanse your heart from the things that caused you to do wrong?"

Danny nodded.

"That prayer was based on God's promise in I John 1:9, *'If we tell Him our sins, He is faithful and we can depend on Him to forgive us of our sins. He will make our lives clean from all sin.'"*

Danny nodded again, hoping he could remember where that promise was in the Bible. He had a feeling that he was going to need it more than just these two times!

"This time, why don't you pray it?" Again Coach bowed his head, reached out his hand, and again Danny took it.

"God, I am really sorry I acted the way I did to Mom last night. I didn't even care about where I spend Christmas this year. That was just meanness. God, I am sorry that I've been thinking I'm better than some other people too. Please forgive me and clean out my heart from all the selfishness and the pride … well as much of it as you can get out … so I won't do that stuff any more. Amen."

When he looked up Coach Adams was nodding and smiling at him. "Amen! Now, about the dreams and the haunted house … you say that all the lights went out when you were in there in the room with the green scarves?"

"Yes, Sir. Then when they came back on, I just left. I know I was being a baby but …"

Coach interrupted. "I don't think you were being a baby. I would have left too!"

"Really?" Danny felt better.

"Now, I don't understand a lot about the devil but I do know that one of the things he does, one of the schemes he works, is to make us afraid. He knew what the decorations at the haunted house were going to be like – they've probably been like that for years – and the lights probably go off at the same time every year. So he put the thoughts of green into your mind through the dream, along with a picture of himself. He prompted someone to get you to go to the haunted house, and then when it matched your dream, you were left with an impression of him being more powerful than he really is. That's what he really wants – to exalt himself instead of God in our minds."

"But ..." Danny started to speak but realized that if he mentioned the ball that hit him or the mouse that chased Maggie, he would be betraying Club secrets. So he just nodded.

Coach Adams went on. "The devil can't do anything in the world without the help of some person because God gave mankind authority in the earth. That's why the devil started at the beginning to get access to man's mind – to get man to use his God–given authority for evil instead of good."

That really made sense to Danny!

"Of course, the devil doesn't want you to go through with your confirmation so he's really coming down heavy on you right now."

Danny wanted to ask more questions but he spotted the clock and saw that it was almost time for the bell so he stood up. "Thank you, Coach Adams. I feel a lot better about everything."

"Anytime, Son." The Coach smiled and turned back to his paperwork.

≈≈≈

To Danny, it seemed a long time since class yesterday. Maggie, Gretchen, David, and Ray were all in a great mood, like they were still feeling the victory over "the command." It didn't seem like they had been through any kind of battle last night like he had. Maybe their hearts weren't filled with pride like his. No, from what Coach Adams said, everybody has that problem. Danny sighed. It was one of those Christian mysteries that he didn't understand.

Danny looked around at his classmates, especially the girls, because Harold had said "she." *One of them is a full-fledged witch. Which one?*

That day at lunch, the Club members didn't get to talk about their victory because Harold Sands came to sit with them.

"Hey, guys," Harold said as he set his tray down on the table across from Danny.

"Hey," said Danny, being polite and trying to hide his disappointment at the interruption of their lunchtime discussions. The two other boys and Gretchen looked up at him and nodded. Maggie didn't say anything and Danny noticed that especially because she was usually so friendly to everyone.

"What's going on?" said Harold.

Nobody said a word. Danny figured that, like himself, all they could think of were forbidden topics.

"What are you getting for Christmas?" Harold tried again.

Ray said, "I'm getting a new bike. I've outgrown my old one."

Harold didn't exactly sneer but you could tell he didn't think that was much of a present.

David added, "I haven't had time to think about it. I'm just now thinking about what I am going to give people."

When Harold looked at Danny, he just shrugged.

Harold smirked. "I'm getting a new computer, my own, not to share, just for me. It will be my very own, in my own room. "

Danny wanted to say something nice but the words stuck in his throat. He couldn't even imagine getting a computer for both Mom and him, much less a computer of his own. Life just wasn't fair.

A warning bell went off somewhere inside him but he ignored it.

"I'm giving my mom a membership in the flower–a–month club." Harold looked very pleased with himself. Harold was the only other kid Danny knew who, like himself, lived alone with his mother. He wondered where Harold came up with money to give his mother a gift like that.

Danny decided that as soon as he could, he would ask him.

That afternoon in study period, the command did not come. For the first time since school started, there was no "Go To Sleep" to combat. Danny didn't know whether he felt relieved or disappointed. He could tell by the looks on the faces of his friends that they didn't know what to think either.

That afternoon he caught up with Harold outside on the walk in front of the school.

"Hey, Harold. Man, I liked that thing you're giving your mom for Christmas. She will get a flower every month all year?"

Harold nodded and looked very pleased with himself.

"How much does it cost?"

Harold looked very important. "A lot. Over a hundred dollars."

"Whoa! That is a lot. How'd you get that much money?"

"I earned it," said Harold.

"Where do you work?" asked Danny.

Harold let out a snort. "Here and there. You interested?"

"Well, yeah. I'd like to get my mom a nice present for Christmas."

"Tell you what," Harold said, "I'll let you in on it if you promise not to tell anybody – not anybody, you hear?"

Danny thought a minute. Last year it would have been easy to promise. There would have been no one to tell. But this year he was part of a Club … a Club that had no secrets from each other. But to be able to buy Mom a Christmas present …

Suddenly he was aware of that little angel and that little devil each speaking in an ear. Then he remembered that Coach Adams had said they were really words battling in his own mind.

"Sorry," he said. "Thanks anyway. I don't keep secrets very well." He turned and went back into the school, walking as fast as he could, his heart pounding. After he got there, he realized he didn't have anything to do there but just wanted to get away before curiosity got the best of him. He opened his locker and stared inside at nothing. Then he did what he should have done before.

"Lord, I want to buy my mom a Christmas present, but I don't have any money. Would You help me?"

When Danny got home that day there was a letter in the mail

just for him from Gramma and Grampa. In the envelope was a check for $25 with a letter explaining that it was not a gift for Danny to buy something for himself but for him to buy something for his mother for Christmas from himself.

"Thank you, God." Danny said fervently. Then he remembered what the Coach had said that morning about praying for others, so he added, "God, please help Harold Sands to really know who You are. If he's in something that he shouldn't be in, help him get out. Amen." But something kept nagging at him.

He bowed his head again. "Lord, forgive me for being jealous of Harold getting a computer. I trust you to give me what I need. Thank you. Amen again."

As he opened his books to do homework, it occurred to him that he should pray for Leo and his sidekicks. He'd do that later. But he couldn't imagine them ever getting nice. That seemed like too much work for even God to do!

Chapter Thirteen

Hate Command

The snow drifted down in huge flakes outside the school windows.

They'd probably have to cancel the Fun To Be One Club meeting that afternoon. The weather had been great all fall and they'd never missed a meeting but today …

At lunch, Danny asked his mom a question and she agreed. When he joined the others at the table, he said, "Mom said we can meet at our place today."

The others looked stunned.

Maggie voiced the question for them all. "You TOLD her? About the Fun to Be One Club?"

"No," Danny said. "I just asked if I could have some of my friends, my church friends, over after school and she said yes."

They all visibly relaxed.

David nodded. "Then that's okay. " He looked at Ray. "What do you think?"

Ray shrugged, "Better than sitting in a cold place on hard ground."

David said, "We've never met anywhere but the Clubhouse."

Maggie smiled at Danny. "It sounds like a great idea to me."

Gretchen nodded. "I'll tell Polly."

Maggie said, "I'll let Kyleigh know and she can tell Scooter. But where will we get together to go to your place?"

Danny said, "By the school sign at the end of the block."

They all nodded, then Maggie said, " Hey, there was no command yesterday. Do you think she has given up?"

David shook his head. "No way."

Harold Sands joined them again and the conversation ended. Right after he sat down, Angela Wicker came to the table too.

Maggie looked over at Danny and rolled her eyes as if to say, "How much torture do we have to put up with?"

≋

That day when the command came, it was not "Go to sleep," it was "Hate!"

It startled Danny. He looked around at the others and they all gave each other 'the look' which told Danny they all heard the command too. He began saying to himself "God is Love. I choose love. I am set apart to share the likeness of His son." He said it over and over until he didn't hear the "hate" command any more.

But he saw that the command had gotten through to some of his classmates, even some of the members. Gretchen squealed as her hair was pulled and she turned back with a terrible glare at Leo. Another girl stomped on the foot of a girl in the row beside her. A sharpened pencil came whizzing through the air and just missed Danny's ear by a fraction.

The command didn't bypass Ms. Gray either.

She broke up an argument between Leo and another boy, then went back to the front of the class and looked out at them all with narrowed eyes. "I have had it with this class. You are the most disgusting students I have ever had the misfortune to teach." Danny could see that she was trembling.

He and Maggie exchanged a quick glance, then suddenly he knew what to do.

Danny started thinking about how Jesus died for every person in the class. Jesus died for Ms. Gray, for Leo, for Harold and Angela, and for every single one of them. "God loves every one of them. No person is the enemy, only the devil. He even loves the person giving the hate command. And Love never fails." Danny began with Ms. Gray, then moved his attention to the far row of desks and thought about how God loved each one seated in them. By the time he got to the end of his own row, things were calm. He looked over at Maggie and noticed that she had been doodling hearts on her paper. He grinned at how they had both known what to do.

≈≈≈

Later at the apartment, they sat on the floor in the living room and discussed the new command. Polly and the younger two children were fascinated by the description of the change in the atmosphere of the class when "Hate" was sent out.

"This one is more dangerous," said Polly. "Somebody could really get hurt."

"Not if we do what Maggie and I did," Danny said. "It worked."

"What do you mean?" asked Maggie.

Danny was puzzled. "Thinking God's love at everybody. I saw you drawing hearts on your paper."

Maggie frowned. "I didn't really do that on purpose. I just found myself doodling it. What were you doing?"

They all looked at Danny, who felt his cheeks grow warm.

"I just, well, I just thought how much God loved each person and how Jesus died for them and how they weren't the enemy, how even the one who was giving the command isn't the enemy."

"It worked." David said thoughtfully. "I was finding myself really angry at the person who was trying to control all our minds. I felt hate toward her. But then it went away as quickly as it came."

Maggie looked up. "Are we sure it's a her? I think it could be a boy."

They all were surprised.

Ray said, "Yeah, we're sure because of what Harold said before he got hit in the head."

Maggie said, "I don't know. Everybody is always against girls."

An outroar from the boys silenced her.

Maggie smiled sheepishly. "Okay, maybe I'm wrong. But there is just so much prejudice against girls – and you know it's true!" She turned to look at David defiantly. "What if Harold was lying? What if it was really a boy?"

Danny thought Maggie just wanted to believe that, so he didn't say anything as the others argued with her.

Then he said, "I think we should tell Coach Adams about the commands."

They all looked at him. "I agree," said David immediately. Danny could tell that this had been discussed before.

"Me too," Ray agreed.

Maggie just looked at the floor and didn't say anything.

Gretchen said, "I don't care."

Polly said, "I've always thought so."

Kyleigh and Scooter both agreed to go along with whatever the others decided.

"Oh, okay!" Maggie said, and wiped away a tear that had escaped from her eye.

What is wrong with Maggie? Danny wondered.

≋≋≋

Confirmation was that Sunday and Danny felt wonderful as he and the others were welcomed into full membership in the church. Some of them, like Danny, chose to be immersed. It felt good to come up out of the water and know that he was a brand new person in Jesus Christ. Afterwards he felt great pride as his mom joined the church too. It was a good day. Danny felt very grateful for all that God had done in just the four short months since they had moved from the city.

The last week of school before Christmas was fun. It seemed like every day there was a program or a party of some kind and it was only a three–day week. The Club met one last time before the holidays, right after the last day of school, and they met at the Clubhouse.

Danny was surprised to see that the place stayed dry through the snow melting all around. There was mud on the way there but the floor of the Clubhouse was fine. The members sat huddled closer together than usual, on their pillows and bundled up in their jackets and gloves.

Polly looked around. "I think we need to each bring a blanket and we could put them … there!" She pointed at a built up area in one corner where hens obviously used to roost. "In plastic, like the pillows."

They all agreed that was a good idea for the winter months. They also agreed that they would talk to Coach Adams right after the holidays.

Even though it was cold in the Clubhouse, Danny felt a warm glow as he looked around at his friends. He, Danny Alcorn, was a part of something – something important and something good. He was accepted by some really nice kids, both boys and girls. He was a member of a church that even kids from other churches wanted to come to and he wasn't having any more nightmares. It was all almost too good to be true.

The Club wasn't going to meet during the Christmas holidays because Polly, Kyleigh, and Gretchen would be gone and the rest all had family coming in again. In fact everyone would be busy except Danny. He brushed aside the disappointment that tried to get back into his mind. Life was good and Christmas would be good even if he and Mom weren't going to fly to Gramma's. He had bought Mom a really good bottle of perfume at the department store at the mall and he knew she would be surprised and happy.

And he, well, he couldn't really think of anything he wanted … that they could afford. Usually there were some movies he begged for, but this year there weren't any out that appealed to him. He guessed he'd probably get new clothes since he was taller and had lost weight, and really needed them. He reminded himself of how lucky … no, blessed … he was and refused to feel sorry for himself in any way.

But there was a little lump in his throat when he told the others goodbye. The two weeks stretching out in front of him looked very empty.

≈≈≈

The next day wasn't as bad as Danny expected. Mom had to work one more day at school and she asked him to put the tree together and put the lights on it and promised that night after she got in from work at the diner, they would decorate and have popcorn and hot chocolate. He turned the radio on to the Christian radio station to listen to while he did the tree, but he really didn't like any of the programs he heard so he turned it off again after about forty-five minutes. He turned on the television but there wasn't anything interesting there either. He put the lights on in silence. In the silence, he heard the command, "Hate."

Danny went over toward the couch and fell to his knees with his head on his arms on the couch cushion. "Please Father, shine through the hate with your love to all the people that it's going out to … and especially, Father, shine through the hate with your love to the person who is sending it out."

Then he felt better and finished the tree without further interruption.

That night he and Mom decorated the tree and watched a rerun of *The Christmas Story* about the boy who wanted a BB gun for Christmas. Danny liked that movie and so did Mom.

When it was over, Mom asked, "Are we going to Christmas Eve service at our church this year?"

Danny grinned. He had forgotten about that. "Yeah!" *Maybe some of the other kids will be there.*

The next few days went quickly as Mom cooked – Christmas stuff: candy and cookies and cake and other things that Gramma usually made. Danny watched movies and read some adventure books – and sampled all the things Mom cooked. He thought if he kept on eating like that, he wouldn't need new clothes after all but would soon be as heavy as he had been before he started walking to school and eating more healthy. Mom got him to help her get the apartment really clean and he started to complain but decided to listen to the angel instead.

Then it was December 23rd. Christmas Eve Eve, Mom called it. At breakfast, Mom had an unusual twinkle in her eye but she didn't say anything. Danny was suspicious.

"What are you smiling about?" he asked.

"Oh, nothing," she said, obviously filled with thoughts of "the nothing" she was smiling about.

Since it was Christmas and secrets were allowed, Danny didn't push her. After lunch, Mom said, "Come on, we're going out."

"Where?" Danny asked as he got his coat out of the closet.

"Oh, just somewhere," she smiled, her eyes twinkling more brightly.

After they had driven for a while and made several unaccustomed turns, Danny realized they were following the signs to the airport.

He looked at his mom. "Mom! The airport?"

She smiled more broadly and nodded.

"Gramma and Grampa?

This time she laughed out loud with joy. "Yes! They are coming for a week."

"YAY!" Danny shouted. He was really glad that he hadn't complained about the cleaning. He was even more glad that he had done a good job.

"You won't mind giving up your room for a week?" Danny had a double bed in the big bedroom and Mom had a single bed in the small bedroom.

"No, I don't mind. I can sleep on the floor."

"It's not that bad. You can sleep on the couch."

"Oh yeah." He was already lost in thoughts of having a whole family going to the Christmas Eve service together.

Gramma and Grampa here. Just like other families. It was going to be a good Christmas.

Chapter Fourteen

Christmas

On Christmas Eve Danny had never been so happy.

Gramma cooked chili just like she did at her own house every year and he was allowed to open one present like every year since he could remember. The service at their church wasn't going to be until eleven that night instead of at seven like at Gramma's church, but going out so late at night made it seem even more special.

It was around 8:30 and the family had just settled down to watch Danny's Christmas Eve present, a movie about Jesus, when a knock came on the door to the apartment.

Danny was surprised when he opened the door and saw Maggie and her family, and some other people he didn't know, standing there. They all had candles in their hands and Maggie said, "We came to sing carols. Is that okay?"

"Sure!" Danny turned back into the apartment. "Mom, Gramma, Grampa!"

When his family joined them, the group in the hallway broke out into song.

Joy to the World, the Lord is come!

Let earth receive her King.
Let every heart prepare Him room
And heaven and nature sing ...

Danny felt like his heart would burst with the joy they were singing about. His family, his best friend, a new family of Christians there to share their music and joy with him! The candlelight glowing in the hallway made it all seem mystical and awesome and he wished the moment would never end.

When the first song was over, Danny's mother invited the group in but they said, "No, thank you," and began singing again.

Silent Night, Holy Night...

Then they sang a verse Danny had never heard before.

Silent Night, Holy Night
Son of God, Love's pure light
Radiant beams from thy Holy Face
With the dawn of redeeming grace.
Jesus, Lord at thy birth,
Jesus, Lord at thy birth.

He felt tears springing into his eyes as goosebumps sprang out on his arms but he couldn't have tears, not here in front of all these people! Then he looked at his Grampa and saw tears flowing down the old man's cheeks. He looked at Maggie and saw tears in her eyes and then he didn't care.

But immediately after the group finished Silent Night, they burst into,

We wish you a Merry Christmas ...
And a Happy New Year!

Maggie pulled four candy canes out from a bag she was carrying and handed them to Danny, his mom, and grandparents. She and her family left in the midst of "thank you's" from Danny's family and " Merry Christmases" all around.

The movie ended just as it was time to leave for the church...or so they thought! When they got there Danny realized they should have left earlier. Every pew was packed and his family had to sit on folding chairs at the back of the sanctuary.

It didn't feel as homey as Christmas Eve at the little country church where Gramma and Grampa went, but it was Danny's own church and he was glad he was there. He was proud when he and his mom and grandparents joined the line in the aisle to receive Holy Communion. Maggie and several members of her family waved and Danny's family waved back.

It was nice to belong!

As they were leaving, Danny was very surprised to see Coach Adams on the sidewalk at the bottom of the steps. He had a big smile on his face and was looking at Danny's Mom.

He turned and saw his mom smile back at the Coach and heard her say, "Why, I didn't know you went to church here. I've never seen you here before."

The coach answered her. "I don't. But my church doesn't have Christmas Eve services, so I come here … if I'm in town." He turned to Danny. "Hi, son. Excited about the big day tomorrow?"

Son! He called me son again. Danny just nodded. *What a night!*

Mom was introducing Gramma and Grampa to the coach and he found out that Mom called the Coach 'Jerry.' Danny had seen the name Gerald on the coach's certificates on the wall in his office but had never heard anybody call him that. It was a shock, especially when it was his own mother.

The adults stood talking a while and Gramma asked the Coach what he did on Christmas and he said that usually he went to his parents who lived in New York State, but this year his parents had gone on a cruise so he was alone. He said he'd probably go to the restaurant at the new hotel on the bypass. Danny saw Gramma nudge Mom and the next thing he knew Mom had invited the Coach to share Christmas dinner with them at four the next afternoon.

"We have a late breakfast," she said, "and then an early dinner and just snack later at night if we get hungry. I hope that time isn't inconvenient for you."

Coach Adams assured them that four o'clock on Christmas

Day was a perfect time to have dinner and he would see them then.

Just before he turned to walk away, Danny's Mom said, "You could come earlier if you want … about three?"

"That will be great!" He laughed. "Believe it or not, I'm great help in the kitchen."

On the way home, Grampa looked at Mom and said, "Well!"

Mom blushed and shrugged her shoulders. "He's a nice man. I'm hoping that he and Danny will be friends."

Then Danny spoke up and told them how Coach Adams was the favorite teacher in the whole school and how he, Danny, liked him very much. He couldn't go into the reasons without telling them a lot of things he had done wrong and it just didn't seem like that was necessary, or even a good thing. But he was very glad that the Coach and Mom were becoming friends; that looked good for the possibility of summer camp at the Fun To Be One Club.

IF we can come up with the money.

When Danny went to bed that night, he smiled when he thought how pleased his mother was going to be the next morning when she opened her bottle of perfume. He realized that it was the first time in his life that he had ever thought about what someone else would receive on Christmas morning instead of what he would get. There really wasn't anything he wanted. "Thank you, God," he said. "Thank you."

The next morning Danny woke up to the smell of bacon frying and he knew pancakes would accompany the crisp strips later on after they had opened presents. That was the traditional Christmas morning breakfast for the four of them and Gramma made the best pancakes in the world! He jumped out of bed, dressed quickly, and joined the adults in the kitchen.

"Merry Christmas!" Grampa smiled at him over the coffee cup that he lowered when Danny entered the room.

"Merry Christmas!" Danny responded. "Merry Christmas everybody!"

Gramma was at the stove and Mom was seated at the table

with her cup of coffee. Danny went and hugged her.

"Your hot chocolate is in the microwave, ready to be heated," she said.

That was the tradition in their family. Hot chocolate and coffee before gifts, and breakfast afterwards. Danny used to resent the time of fellowship and prayer before going to the Christmas tree but this Christmas was different.

Grampa led them in prayer. "Lord, thank You for this day, for the reminder that You became a baby to become one with us in this fallen world so that we could become one with You in eternity. Thank you for Your generosity that flows through us at this season. Help us to recognize You as the Giver of all gifts and appreciate each other as part of Your grand idea in Creation. In Jesus' Name, Amen."

In a few minutes, they went into the living room and Danny got to hand out the gifts under the tree.

Grampa got a nice pair of leather gloves and some thick socks from Mom and Danny, and they gave Gramma a soft nightgown. Grampa had given Gramma a new Bible and some dusting powder – the kind he gave her every year. Gramma gave Grampa a heavy jacket.

Mom and Danny both got nice winter coats from Gramma and Grampa, and Danny got several shirts and slacks from his mom. Mom was as excited as he hoped when she opened the perfume from him.

Danny's stocking was fun as always with little games and candy and certificates to McDonalds. This year there was a little box with Bible verses in it and some pencils that said, "Smile, Jesus loves you" on them.

When he'd finished looking through the stocking, Grampa said, "What is that box over there near the window?"

Danny looked and there was a big box half hidden by the drapery. He was surprised that he hadn't seen it before and decided that Grampa must have moved it out from behind the curtain while he was examining his stocking.

Danny walked over to the box and saw the card, "To Danny, with love from Mom and Gramma and Grampa."

His hands were a little trembley when he tore the paper off and he sat back on his heels and just stared when he saw the box. It was a computer! He turned and looked at his family in disbelief.

"Don't you like it?" Mom grinned at him.

"Like it?" Danny found he could move again. "Like it? I LOVE it! It's the best! But ... but how?

Gramma said softly, "Grampa and I sold off a couple of acres of land this fall...we'll hardly miss it and a man really wanted it. And well, we thought you are getting to the age when you will need a computer for schoolwork. I mean, everybody has them these days."

Danny ran to her and hugged her and then turned to Grampa and hugged him too.

He looked at Mom. Her name had been on the card too.

She smiled. "My part is internet hookup. If you are going to be able to do research on the computer, you'll need to be able to get on the internet. I'm going to pay that every month."

Danny was speechless. He just went and hugged her too.

"But I don't know how to hook it up."

Mom laughed. "Well, it's kind of funny. I had already asked Coach Adams if he knew about computers and he offered to come over during the holidays and hook it up for you. So, since he is coming to dinner today, maybe he'll be able to do it now. That's one reason I suggested he come early."

"Wow!"

The Coach arrived promptly at three and apologized for not having presents to bring with him.

"We don't have any for you either. It's gift enough to have your company ... and your help with Danny's new computer." Mom smiled at the Coach in a way that Danny had never seen her smile at anybody. *Whoa! Maybe ...*

Danny and Coach Adams worked for about thirty minutes in Danny's room clearing off some space on the desk and setting up the computer and the monitor that Mom had hidden in her room. Then the Coach announced that he was going to help out in the kitchen and they would finish up after dinner.

Christmas dinner tasted better than it ever had and Danny decided it was because of the people he was with … and because of Jesus. He was seated in between Coach Adams and his mom and when they all held hands while Grampa said the blessing, it felt so good, like a real family with a mom *and* a dad.

After dinner, Grampa and Gramma fell asleep sitting up on the couch in the living room watching some Christmas music program. Coach helped Mom with the dishes and then they joined Danny in his room. By the time Coach Adams left, everything was working except the internet and a program the Coach said he would bring by … he looked at Mom and asked, "When?"

Mom blushed and said, "Tomorrow?"

Chapter Fifteen

Coach Adams

All the other Fun To Be One Club kids seemed as excited to be back at school after the holidays as Danny. They talked by phone ahead of time and decided the club meeting would be after school that first day. They all agreed to dress extra warmly and pray at the meeting for God's solution as to how to get blankets to take there without their parents wondering about their meetings. So far the others, like Danny, had just said that they were meeting after school with church friends but didn't say where those meetings took place. Even Coach Adams didn't know where the Clubhouse was located.

But first they had to get through the school day.

Harold Sands joined Maggie, David, Ray, Gretchen, and Danny again at lunch and bragged about his new "just for me" computer. Danny almost bit his tongue to keep from blurting out his own news.

Finally Harold turned to him with a sneer and said, "What did Santa bring you, Alcorn?"

Danny tried not to gloat as he answered as casually as he could manage, "Oh, I got the same thing you did ... a computer for my room." He knew it probably wasn't very Christian of him to enjoy the crestfallen look on Harold's face.

The others at the table began congratulating him, and Harold took his tray to another table, to the relief of them all.

Danny wasn't sure if he should say anything but he did anyway.

"Coach Adams got the computer up and running for me."

"Neat!" Maggie seemed surprised. "How did that happen?"

"My mom asked him before Christmas if he would do it sometime and then we saw him at church Christmas Eve and he came for Christmas dinner."

"You are lucky!" Ray gave him a thumbs up.

"Not lucky, blessed," David corrected him.

"Yeah," agreed Danny. "Really blessed. It was the best Christmas ever. Coach Adams came over a couple of times. I think he and Mom kind of like each other. But don't say anything to the other kids."

They all promised they wouldn't.

It had been several weeks since they had to fight any signals from whoever was sending them but the "Hate" command came more strongly than ever in the classroom that afternoon.

This time all five knew what to do and this time there was no outbreak of anger or violence.

When school was over, they all walked together to the clubhouse. The circle they formed was again tighter than usual because they were huddling together to help keep warm.

"Okay," David began after opening with prayer for guidance from the Holy Spirit.

"I think the first thing we need to do is to decide how to tell the Coach about the commands."

"I think so too." Polly nodded enthusiastically.

"Should it be all of us or just one of us?" Scooter's question surprised Danny because usually the younger boy didn't talk at all.

David looked around at the group. "What does everybody

think?"

Danny was the first to speak. "I think we should all talk to him."

Polly, Gretchen, and Kyleigh all spoke at the same time. "Me too!"

Scooter just nodded.

David looked at Maggie. "Maggie, what do you think?"

She shook her head. "I don't care."

Danny remembered that she hadn't wanted to tell the Coach at all. But he knew she would go along with whatever the group decided.

David asked, "Will all in favor of meeting with Coach Adams as a group raise your right hand?"

David, Polly, Gretchen, Ray, Kyleigh, Scooter, and Danny all raised their hands immediately and a few seconds later Maggie's hand went up too.

David volunteered to set up the meeting and they then moved on to the topic of blankets.

Nobody could think of a way to ask for blankets without explaining about the Clubhouse, and they didn't want to do that because the parents might tell them they couldn't come here.

David said, "I heard somebody say one time that it's easier to get forgiveness than permission."

That didn't seem exactly right to Danny. But David was their leader and knew a lot more than Danny did.

Polly admitted that the secrecy made her uncomfortable but since she really didn't think they were doing anything wrong, she agreed that it was better to just not mention the Clubhouse.

"If we wanted to, I know my mom wouldn't mind if we met at our apartment in the wintertime. She works after school and wouldn't be there." Danny looked around to see if the group was at all interested in his offer.

Nobody said anything for a minute and then David nodded.

"That would be a good thing for the cold weather times. It would be a good place to talk to Coach Adams too."

So it was agreed unanimously that as soon as Danny cleared it with his mother that they could meet there regularly, David would ask the Coach if he could meet them there one afternoon.

≈≈≈

The homemade brownies Mom baked for the occasion were sitting in a pan on the kitchen counter and the Club kids fell on them with great enthusiasm.

"Maybe we should have waited for Coach Adams," Polly said, right before she washed down her last bite with a swallow of milk.

"We saved some for him." Danny pointed to the plate.

"Right." Ray eyed the plate greedily.

"Right!" Kyleigh moved over in front of the counter as if to protect the Coach's snack and they all laughed.

Just then they heard a knock on the front door and Danny let Coach Adams in.

They all gathered around the table and watched while he ate the brownies and drank the glass of milk that Polly poured for him. The talk then was about the volleyball teams, as if by an unspoken agreement that the serious discussion would wait 'til later.

After everyone pitched in to clean up, they went into the living room. Coach Adams sat in the recliner and the others settled themselves around him on the couch and the floor.

"Okay, what's this about?"

Danny immediately looked at David, and realized that the other kids were doing the same thing.

David nodded. "Well, it sounds kind of weird, telling a grown up. But we think … no, Sir, we *know* that there is something really bad going on in Ms. Gray's class." He paused for a few seconds. "Witchcraft kind of bad stuff."

Coach Adams didn't say anything but he didn't look shocked, just nodded encouragingly at David.

"It started the very first day of school. We all heard in our minds, like a, well, we call it the command, 'go to sleep' and every one of us felt sleepy all of a sudden. But we didn't, none of us, go to sleep I mean. We didn't go to sleep but lots of other kids did, everybody else did that first day."

Danny interrupted. "I did, later. It was a couple of weeks later and I did go to sleep when the command came."

David said, "Yeah, I was going to get you to tell about that." He nodded for Danny to continue.

"That night, after I went to sleep in school I had a really bad nightmare. You know, I told you about it."

Coach Adams nodded and Danny could see the other kids looking at each other.

"I didn't tell him about any of the witchcraft stuff," he promised them. "I just told him about my nightmares and something else that happened."

"That's right." Coach Adams assured the group. "Danny hasn't mentioned any of the things you've told me here. But you say that is when your nightmares started?"

"Yes, Sir, that night after I went to sleep in class."

Polly spoke up. "We think that when Danny gave into the command, it let something in his head. He heard the command at home once too."

David added, "But Danny learned how to reject the command. I mean he really learned. He was the one who suggested that we all pray, even the ones not in our class. We wrote out a prayer."

"I brought it." Polly pulled a paper out of her jeans and handed it to Coach Adams.

He took the paper, read it, and then nodded. "I like this. You kids recognize that it's dangerous to just fight with your minds. That's good!" Then he looked back at David, who continued.

"The command changed right before the holidays. Instead of 'go to sleep,' it was 'hate.'"

Maggie spoke for the first time. "Coach Adams, Danny really fought that. I felt really angry when that command came, and people in the room started acting awful, even Ms. Gray. But then I found myself feeling love and doodling hearts on my paper. Everybody calmed down in a few minutes. We found out later that

Danny started thinking about how God loves everybody in the classroom and how Jesus died for them."

David resumed the story. "So the next time that hate command came, we all prayed that way."

Maggie said, "But that's not all! Tell him about the mouse!"

"But first about the basketball," Ray protested.

Danny, Maggie, and Ray all started talking at the same time, then David raised his hand and the others followed suit.

Coach Adams smiled, "You kids really are something ... you know how to keep yourselves in order! Now, one at a time ... who's first?'

David said, "It should be Danny because he's the one who got hit first."

Danny reminded Coach Adams about the day that both he and Harold had been hit with basketballs. He told him what Harold had said right before he was hit and how Harold hadn't remembered anything about the class afterwards.

"Yes," said the Coach thoughtfully. "I wondered about that."

"And now the mouse?" Maggie appeared to have gotten over her reluctance to share with Coach Adams and was now eager to tell him about her adventure. Danny guessed she'd thought he wouldn't take them seriously.

The Coach laughed at the picture of a class gone "mouse mad." This time even Maggie laughed too.

Coach Adams asked a lot of questions about who did or did not fall asleep at that command – who did or did not react to the "hate" suggestion.

Then he asked them who each of them thought was the perpetrator of the suggestions.

Kyleigh and Scooter both just shrugged their shoulders.

Polly said that she thought it was Angela Wicker.

Maggie agreed, and Gretchen said maybe, but she really thought it was Leo.

David said, "No way. He's not smart enough. I think it could be Angela or maybe Cliff Franklin."

At that the others looked at him with surprise. He'd never mentioned that boy before.

"I know!" He shook his head. "Cliff never says or does much of anything but he reads a lot and he may have been studying mind control and stuff like that."

Ray said he didn't have a clue and Danny said the same thing.

Coach Adams closed with a prayer for them and as he was leaving, he turned at the doorway and said, "You kids are doing a good job. Just keep trusting Jesus and follow the promptings of the Holy Spirit. Fight the good fight of faith and love for the rest of your classmates. Pray for the person who has chosen, well, as they would say in Star Wars, the dark side."

They all agreed that they would.

When he had gone, they just looked at each other.

Polly had a frown on her face. "Well, did that do any good?"

Maggie said, "I feel better now that a grown up knows about it. Especially since he thinks we're doing the right thing. I was afraid he'd think we're crazy."

David laughed. "Your roles have switched, huh, girls?"

Both Polly and Maggie laughed.

Maggie said, "Mine has. I am really glad that you all insisted we tell him."

"Me too," said Polly. "I was just hoping he would have an immediate answer, I guess."

"Give him time," David advised.

Chapter Sixteen

Angela Wicker

Danny was walking down the school hallway behind Leo and Eddie and couldn't help overhearing their conversation.

"I can't believe he's gone!" Leo sounded angry.

"Where are we going to get the stuff?"

"Shh. I don't know. I'll ask around and find out. Some of the older guys will know."

"We're going to miss ol' Dirty Drake," Eddie said sadly. "I wonder if he quit or got fired?"

Danny knew without asking. He was sure the information he gave Coach had caused Mr. Drake to lose his job.

Right after school Danny went to the Coach's office and found that he had a few minutes to spare.

"Yes," Coach Adams admitted. "I suggested a search of his office and everything you reported was proven. I was able to do it without revealing my source of information. It was a good thing you told me about it, Son. There were some pretty bad things in there and he was messing up the lives of a lot of kids."

"Then," Danny hesitated, "this is what is bothering me. If it was a good thing that I told you about the bottle, was it God that made me look in the drawer? I told God I was sorry for looking in there because I thought it was wrong."

The Coach looked at Danny thoughtfully. "Danny, you are astute, have good judgment, far beyond your years. That is a good question. And a very deep one. I don't have all the answers, Son, but I know this. God knows everything that we are going to do, every choice we will make. He will cause all things to work for good for those who love Him, and who are called for His purpose. No, He didn't make you want to see what the other boys were buying from Mr. Drake, but He knew you were going to look, and when you did, He led you to eventually come to me and report it."

Danny remembered thinking about the angel and devil on his shoulders, and how he chose the angel when he decided to tell about snooping. He nodded.

"But, Sir, what about Mr. Drake? He doesn't have a job now. What if he starts stealing or something? Won't that be my fault?"

Coach Adams smiled. "Well, I guess it would be my fault as much as yours, maybe more. I'm the one who reported his behavior to the school system. What do you think? Should I feel guilty?"

Danny shook his head. "No, you were just protecting us kids."

"What were you doing?"

Danny grinned. "The same thing, I guess. Yeah, the same thing."

"Danny, Mr. Drake is responsible for his own choices ... and his own consequences. He could have decided to follow the rules and be a good example for the kids in the school but he didn't. Now he has another choice. He can choose to straighten up and find another job and follow the rules there, or he can make wrong choices again. Whatever happens will be a consequence of what he decides. Just like what happened here was a consequence of his choice."

Danny breathed a sigh of relief. "That makes sense." He got out of the chair and held out his hand. "Thank you, Sir."

The two shook hands and then Coach Adams said, "I would

like to ask you some more questions about the day you were hit with the basketball. I don't have time right now but maybe later on this afternoon. Would you mind if I came by the apartment?"

"No! But ... I don't want Mom ... I mean, the others would be mad if we let Mom know about the commands and stuff."

Coach shook his head. "No, I won't betray their trust. I was going to come by after practice while she is still at work at the restaurant. She gets off at eight, right?"

"Right. Okay, that'll be great. See you then."

There was no club meeting that afternoon and his friends were already gone by the time Danny went outside. Angela Wicker was leaving the school at the same time he did.

At first, they didn't say anything but it felt kind of awkward, walking down the sidewalk four feet apart, without speaking.

Danny broke the silence, "Did you have a good Christmas?"

Angela turned and looked surprised. That puzzled Danny because surely she had known he was right behind her. Or was she surprised that he spoke?

"I suppose." She turned back around and walked on. But Danny decided to make her have a conversation with him. Maybe Maggie and Polly were right. Maybe she was the one giving the commands, even if she was a church person. Maybe if he talked to her, he would be able to have a better idea if she was doing witchcraft.

"I noticed you reading the witch books last fall. Were they good?"

Angela turned around again and looked at him with disgust. "Yes, they were good. Haven't you read them?"

Danny shook his head. "Nope. I was in confirmation classes and reading the Bible and the other church stuff. Should I read them?" By this time, Danny was walking beside her.

She shrugged. "How should I know?"

"I remember you said that the Haunted House and the church party at Halloween were baby stuff. So I just wondered if those books were grown-up stuff."

At that, Angela gave a short laugh and seemed to relax. "Good point. I liked them because they are funny. They make fun of stupid people so I don't know if you would like them or not. They are fantasy and in that way, I guess they are like the Haunted House and the Halloween Alternative party … make-believe, kid stuff. But … well they are grown-up in the kind of humor they have in them and I liked them."

"I liked the church party. It wasn't make-believe or kid stuff. It was fun for both kids and grown-ups. You should have tried it."

Angela turned to look at him with narrowed eyes. "You're strange, Danny Alcorn. You're not like the other kids."

Danny felt a pang in his midsection. He had always known that he was different, he had never fit in, but the Fun To Be One Club kids had taken him in and he had not felt that difference and loneliness for months. Now all of a sudden Angela reminded him of all his weaknesses.

"I know," he said sadly. "I'm sorry I bothered you." He walked on quickly, wanting to kick himself for opening a conversation with the prettiest girl in school. *What did I expect?*

"Danny?" Angela's voice was slightly breathless, like she was also walking quickly, to catch up with him. "Danny?"

He slowed down and looked back. She was trying to catch up with him!

"Danny, wait!" He stopped until she caught up.

"I didn't mean that in a bad way. I meant that you are more grown up in a lot of ways than the other kids. I've watched you all year and listened to you in class. You ask good questions and I think you are smart."

Danny was speechless.

Angela continued, "The reason I said what I did, is that most other kids wouldn't have said that I should have gone to the party. That was brave of you. Most of the kids don't even talk to me."

Danny knew they didn't say anything to her because Angela aways acted like she knew she was smarter than the others in the class and she said things to put the other kids down all the time.

But he didn't tell Angela that.

Instead he said, "I didn't think you ever wanted to talk." He laughed. "But I decided to make you talk to me anyway."

Angela smiled. When she did, Danny thought she was prettier than ever, probably the prettiest girl in the whole town, not just the school.

"I'm glad you made me talk, Danny." Her voice was softer than he'd ever heard it.

They came to a crossing and realized that they were going separate ways from that point on.

Danny said, "Well, I'm glad we talked too. Maybe we can talk again sometime."

Angela nodded and waved goodbye before she turned the corner.

Danny stood there a minute before crossing the street. *Maybe we can talk again sometime? What a stupid thing to say!!!*

But Angela didn't think he was stupid. She thought he was smart! Danny really hoped more than ever that she was not the one giving the commands.

≈≈≈

It was a little after six when Coach knocked on the door to the apartment.

Danny offered him a sandwich and some chips and he accepted immediately. Danny was glad to have company for supper and Coach Adams said he was glad to have supper after a long day of physical exertion.

After they ate and cleaned up what little mess they made, they went into the living room. Coach took the recliner again and Danny sat on the couch.

"Okay, I want to get it clear in my mind exactly what happened that day with the basketball. I remember you and Harold Sands both getting hit but I didn't know anything strange was behind it all. That was the day I met your mom."

Danny told again how Leo kicked the ball and hit him, and that Harold came up to Danny and said, "She made him do it, I saw her" before another basketball hit Harold and knocked him out.

"Where were you when that happened?"

"I was sitting on the bleacher like you told me, holding my head down. You went over to talk to Leo."

Coach Adams was quiet and looked like he was thinking back on the scene. He nodded. "Okay."

Then to Danny's surprise, he completely changed the subject. "Tell me about Angela Wicker."

Danny could feel his face getting red.

"What do you mean?"

"Well, she seems to be the favorite choice for the one sending the commands. You didn't have a suspect but I wanted you to tell me why the others would think she was the one."

"She read the witch books … you know, the ones that are so popular."

Coach nodded.

"She doesn't seem to have any friends. I don't think she is the one though, she goes to church."

"I wish going to church was proof that a person was godly but I'm afraid that just isn't true." The Coach sounded sad when he said it.

"Well, I don't think Angela is the one!" Danny realized that he really didn't think she was guilty. It wasn't because she was pretty or because she thought he was smart. It was because it just didn't feel right to him inside. But he didn't know how to explain that to anybody.

Coach Adams changed the subject again. "Tell me about the time when you all fought the command to sleep and it worked for the whole class."

Danny told him and the Coach asked, "Who was the last one to wake up?"

Danny thought for a minute and then said, "Harold Sands."

Coach Adams nodded again but didn't ask any more questions about the strange things going on at school.

Instead, he shifted in the chair and looked a little embarrassed.

"Danny, I want to ask you something and I want you to be honest with me."

"Yes Sir?"

"Would it bother you … I mean, would it be okay … would you care if I asked your mother out on a date?"

Danny grinned. "No Sir! I've kind of been hoping that you would."

They laughed together in relief that the subject was out in the open. But they didn't talk about it any more.

They talked about what Danny was learning at school until they heard a key being turned in the front door and Danny's Mom opened it and came in.

She looked surprised and happy when she saw Coach Adams there with Danny.

Chapter Seventeen

A Need to Belong

Danny stuffed his jacket inside his backpack and saw that the others had done the same thing, or were carrying theirs. The Club kids were on their way to Danny's apartment on that unseasonably warm January day.

"You know, it's warm enough to go to the Clubhouse today." Maggie said what Danny was thinking. He thought the rest were probably thinking the same thing but didn't want to hurt his feelings by saying they'd rather go there than to his place.

Danny spoke up quickly. "Why don't you all go on and I'll run home and get the cookies Mom left for us and meet you there."

"Great!" David waved as Danny separated from the group and sped up his walking pace.

He hadn't gone very far when he saw Harold Sands step out from behind some bushes that made a hedge around a front yard. Danny didn't think that was where Harold lived and wondered what the other boy had been doing there.

"Where are your friends off to?" Harold's voice was taunting, and Danny felt a chill run through his stomach. *Surely Harold didn't know about the Clubhouse!* Then Danny relaxed. Harold couldn't know about it – they hadn't met there for a long time and he would have said something before now if he had discovered it.

"What do you mean?"

"I see you leave together all the time. Usually you all go together to your place. Why aren't they going with you today?"

Danny didn't know what to say, or what to do. He thought a quick prayer and the answer – if it was an answer to his prayer – came in the form of a thought about a sports concept. He decided to take the offense instead of the defense. He took a step toward Harold and put a frown on his face.

"Have you been following us?" He glared at his classmate.

He was shocked at the scared look on Harold's face. The boy backed up a couple of steps and held up one hand.

"Hey man, I don't want trouble. I don't follow anybody. I just saw you a couple of times and was surprised that they didn't come with you today. That's all."

Danny knew that wasn't all. He knew then that Harold had been hiding behind the hedge in order to hear their conversation when they walked by. His eyes narrowed. *Nosy little sneak!* But then a picture of himself less than four months ago arose in his mind. Hadn't he followed the kids to the Clubhouse himself? And hadn't it been not just curiosity, but because he felt left out?

Suddenly he changed his expression and his tone of voice.

"That's okay. Sometimes some of us church kids get together to talk about church stuff, you know, the Bible and all."

He saw Harold's lip curl and his nose wrinkle up.

"That's boring."

Danny smiled. "Not to us. See ya, Harold." He walked on, leaving the boy standing on the sidewalk. He didn't look back til he came to a street crossing and he saw Harold turning the corner and going the opposite way from the Fun To Be One Clubhouse. Danny breathed a sigh of relief.

≈≈≈

"That's scary," Maggie was the first one who spoke after

Danny told them about Harold. They were all seated around the floor of the Clubhouse on their pillows. It wasn't quite as warm there as the outside weather had seemed to guarantee. When Danny got there with the cookies the others told him they almost changed their minds and joined him at the house. After a few minutes on his own pillow, through which the cold ground quickly penetrated, he saw what they meant.

Danny shook his head. "I did the same thing, remember?"

Every other voice there said, "WHAT?"

Maggie blushed. "Sorry, guys. I didn't tell you that part when I told you that I brought him here. Danny followed us one day before that, and heard us in here talking. I was really angry at first when he told me, but then I knew the King wanted him to be a part of us so, well, I didn't want you all to get mad at him too."

"What about the No Secrets rule?" Scooter looked upset.

"I'm sorry. I guess I broke it but I really never thought again about him doing that, not after that first day. Really!"

Danny added, "I'm sorry too. I ask you all to forgive me for spying. That's what God reminded me of today when I was so mad at Harold. I remembered it wasn't just curiosity … it was that I wanted so much to belong in your group. But then after I heard what you were talking about, it didn't seem very exciting to me. But I felt awful, that I had spied on you." He looked around at the serious faces.

David broke the uncomfortable silence. "Of course we forgive you." He looked around at the others who nodded in agreement. Then he narrowed his eyes and shook his head. "You too, Maggie." He grinned at her before turning back to Danny.

"You wouldn't believe how determined she was to bring you into the Club."

Maggie said quietly, "I knew he belonged here."

Ray spoke up, "But this brings up a whole new problem. If people are noticing us leave together, there may be others who follow us. We're just lucky … er, blessed … that Harold followed us going to Danny's instead of coming here."

"That's right," agreed Polly.

"So what do we do?" Maggie sounded worried.

Ray answered. "Come separately."

The solution was so simple that they all laughed.

"Now, down to business. Wait, first let's pray." David turned to Danny. "We were going to wait 'til you got here and then when you told us about Harold I forgot." He bowed his head. "Father here we are again, gathered in Jesus' Name, like He said, so He is here with us and we are asking that You guide our talk and help us to feel Your Love and show us anything we need to know. In Jesus' Name, Amen."

Kyleigh was the first to speak, which surprised Danny because she rarely said anything. "What is going on in your classroom? About the commands, I mean."

Maggie said, "It's kind of strange; they are not...well, not as strong or something. It's like the person is still saying go to sleep to our minds but almost like it's a habit and they don't really care." She looked around at the others who were in Ms. Gray's class. They nodded in agreement.

"I wonder what happened?" asked Polly.

"Prayer," said Danny. "I mean we've been praying for whoever is doing it, haven't we? That's got to be the answer."

Maggie looked uncomfortable. "I forgot. I haven't been praying for them, just praying against what they were doing."

Kyleigh spoke up again. "I have. That's why I wondered."

"Me too," said Polly.

"Sometimes I do but mostly I forget," Gretchen admitted.

"Yeah," added Ray.

"Me too," said Scooter. Then he confessed. "That's a lie. I'm like Maggie, I haven't prayed for her at all, just against what she's doing."

"I've been thinking about that," said Danny. "I'm not sure that it's a girl."

Maggie blurted out, "But Harold said it was a girl."

"Why should we believe everything Harold Sands says?"

Danny shook his head. "He lied today about spying on us and I think he might have been either lying or just trying to make himself look important when he told me that about the basketball."

"He sure does try to make himself look important!" Gretchen wrinkled her nose.

Danny said, "Why don't we pray for the person, who ever it is, right now, while we're together? Let's ask God to, well, to get them to be a Christian."

"Save 'em. We'll ask God to save her ... or him." Ray provided the phrase that Danny had been searching for. His church didn't use the expression 'save' but it sure fit. He knew he was saved from the life he lived just five months ago.

"Okay." David bowed his head again. "Lord, we hold up the person who has been responsible for all the sleep and hate commands and for the basketball and mouse things. We thank you that Jesus died for them as much as He did for us. We ask you to show them that you love them. Help them be excited about you instead of excited about witchcraft. Help them see how you need them working for the Kingdom instead of them feeling good about themselves because of having power over people's minds. Save them, Lord, please. Ame ... oh, and Lord, we also hold up Harold Sands to you. He goes to church, Lord, but he doesn't know You. We ask you to save him too. In Jesus' Name, Amen."

Danny ended up walking home with Maggie and he thanked her for not telling the others about his spying.

She said, "I really was telling the truth. I didn't think about it after that first day. I wasn't keeping a secret on purpose."

"Good." Danny smiled. "I remembered that when I was talking to Harold. I couldn't be real mad at him because I kept thinking that maybe he is like me, he just needs friends."

Maggie sneered. "I sure hope God doesn't tell us we have to have *him* in the Fun To Be One Club."

Maggie turned off to go to her street and Danny went on until he remembered that he had left Mom's plate at the Clubhouse.

When he was just inside the door, he saw Kyleigh, and she was crying. It was too late to leave without being seen, so, feeling awkward, he went over to her and stood beside her as she sat on the ledge where the supplies were kept.

"I guess you don't want to talk about it or you would have told the others. I'm sorry to bother you; I forgot Mom's plate."

Kyleigh wiped away a tear and said, "It's okay. I think I'd like to tell you. I think you'd understand. I heard my mom and dad talking last night and I think they are going to get a divorce. They fight a lot and I have prayed so hard. That's why I wanted to know about the commands, the person really. It just seems like my prayers don't work."

"Don't say that! Don't ever say that. Yes, your prayers work because Jesus said they do. See, your prayers are working for the person who is doing the witchcraft. They just aren't as interested."

Kyleigh nodded. "Okay, good. But they aren't working for my mom and dad."

"You don't know that," Danny answered. "You don't know what God is doing that you can't see yet."

She smiled at him shyly. "Thank you, Danny. You're right. I won't give up. Thank you."

"You're welcome."

Danny got the plate and this time he made it all the way home.

When Mom came in that night, she brought Danny a hamburger and French fries. He was glad because he hadn't eaten anything since the cookies at the Clubhouse.

Mom sat at the kitchen table with him while he ate. "Well, guess what?"

"Hmm?" Danny's mouth was full of hamburger.

"Coach Adams came and ate at the restaurant tonight. He asked if he could come to church with us Sunday and take us out to eat lunch afterwards."

Danny gave a thumbs–up as he hastily swallowed the mouthful.

"Cool!"

"Yes, very cool. I really like him, Danny. I like him a lot."

"He likes you too. He asked me if I would mind if he asked you on a date."

"I know. He told me." Mom gave a little giggle. "That's kind of funny. In old-fashioned times men asked fathers if they could date their daughters. Now he's asking my son if he can date his mother."

"And your son says YES!"

Mom got up and hugged Danny. "Life has changed so much for us this past six months. Isn't God good?"

Danny nodded, mouth full of French fries.

≈≈≈

Danny walked in the boy's restroom at school that next day and saw Leo and Eddie, and Harold. Harold was on the ground with Eddie sitting on him and Leo standing above. A fierce anger came over Danny.

"That's enough, Leo." He said it in a quiet but firm voice that surprised himself.

Evidently it surprised Leo too because the bully turned around and looked Danny right in the eye. They just stared at each other for what seemed to Danny a long, long time. Then Leo said, "Oh come on, Bugger. This shrimp isn't worth it."

The two left. Harold got up off the floor and looked at Danny with respect in his eyes.

"Thanks," he said.

Chapter Eighteen

Valentine Dance

Ms. Gray made two announcements that morning. The first was that their grade and the ones above and below them would start changing classes at the first of March. She said that the school officials intended to begin that after Christmas holidays but everything just hadn't gotten worked out until now. The other announcement was that the school was having a Valentine Dance for those three grades. It would be held in the gymnasium on the Friday night closest to Valentine's Day.

Danny and Maggie exchanged glances. This was interesting!

At lunch that day, the talk was all about the school news. Danny was glad that they didn't have important Fun To Be One Club business to discuss since both Angela Wicker and Harold Sands joined them at their regular table.

Harold didn't say much, which was unusual. Mostly Harold liked to brag about things but not today. Danny figured it was because of what happened in the restroom the day before.

Angela, who usually didn't say anything, was talking about the new school schedule.

"I believe they are trying to catch up with the other schools across the state, treating us more like middle schoolers even if we are still in the same building as the grade school. And the dance too! I don't think they have ever had a dance before."

Gretchen smiled at Angela. "It is nice that they are treating us more like, well, like we are more grown up than the younger kids. I wonder how they will divide the classes?"

Angela said, "I hope they divide us into scholastic achievement groups, where the more advanced students are not held back by the slower ones. But if the smart kids in the class behind us are in with us, that would still hold us back."

Danny felt a movement of fear in his stomach. Suppose he got put in a class with all the kids who were slow? If they based it on all his years in school and the grades he had earned, that would happen for sure. He looked around the table and saw that all the others were nodding, except Maggie. Maggie was looking at Angela in a way that made Danny think that if he were Angela he wouldn't want to meet up with Maggie alone behind the school.

Maggie interrupted, "Well, I like our class the way it is and I don't want to change classes."

Danny agreed with her but he didn't say anything. *Coward!* He fussed at himself.

Gretchen changed the subject. "So, is everybody going to the Valentine's Day dance?"

They all said they guessed so, except Danny.

Angela asked, "Aren't you going to the dance, Danny?"

He shrugged his shoulders. "I can't dance."

Suddenly Harold was more like himself again. He snorted. "You can't dance?"

Danny looked at him for a minute before he answered. "No, I can't dance. So I don't see any sense in going to a dance."

Angela said, "You can learn, Danny. I would teach you."

Maggie got up, took her tray, and left the table.

≋≋

That afternoon, the command returned. Only this time it didn't say "go to sleep" or "hate." It said, "dance." Danny almost laughed because he felt a desire to get up and skip around. But immediately after that he remembered something he read in the Bible the night before, "There is a time for everything under the sun ... a time to dance." This time ... here in the middle of Ms. Gray's classroom during school hours – was NOT a time for dancing. So Danny just started praying, "Lord help everyone not dance."

He had closed his eyes for a minute to concentrate on his prayer and when he opened them, he saw Maggie obviously trying to get his attention by swinging her arm beside the desk where Ms. Gray couldn't see. When he looked at her, he saw that Maggie had an excited and triumphant look on her face. She nodded.

Did Maggie know who was giving the commands?

As soon as class was dismissed that afternoon, Maggie pulled him aside in the hallway. "Harold was right. It is a HER."

"Who?"

"It's Angela Wicker," Maggie announced triumphantly.

Danny thought he must have looked as unbelieving as he felt because Maggie's eyes flashed anger.

"It is! If you think about it, even her name fits."

"Her name? Angela? I thought Angela meant angel."

"No, not her first name. Wicker, get it? Wicker for wicked, and most important Wicker, like Wicca – witchcraft! Even the Angela part fits too... there are fallen angels, you know."

Danny shook his head. "I don't think ..."

Maggie's eyes narrowed. "You don't want to think! But it's true anyway."

"How do you know?"

"It just came to me in class. I heard the dance command and I knew. She wants you to learn to dance, she even said she would teach you. Well, she started already, trying to teach you, I mean."

Danny shook his head again. "I really don't think it's Angela. I walked part of the way home with her the other day and ..."

"Oh! So she's your girlfriend now?" Maggie's voice was

sarcastic.

"No!" Danny glared at her. "I don't have a girlfriend and don't want one. What I was going to say was that I prayed and asked the Lord to show me if she was the one, because some of you thought so. I just was sure inside that she wasn't."

Maggie just looked at him a long time, then said, "Hmph," and marched away, leaving Danny standing alone wondering what made her so mad at him.

≈≈≈

On the night of the Valentine's Dance, the air was crisp but not too cold. It reminded Danny more of a fall night than a winter one. His mom was going to chaperone and so was Coach Adams. He thought that Coach got her put on the chaperone team. She asked Danny if he minded her being there and he said no, why should he?

Mom laughed and said, "The day will come …!"

Coach Adams drove them to school so Danny got there about half an hour earlier than the other kids. He helped carry refreshments from the kitchen to the gym where the dance was going to be. There was a big punch bowl with pink punch in it and heart shaped cookies with red and white icing on them. He, Mom, and another woman who worked in the kitchen put them on the table that had a red cover on it. They also put paper cups, plates, and napkins out on the table.

The gym was all decorated with red and white crepe paper streamers, and hearts. There was an old-fashioned jukebox, like at Arnolds on the old TV show reruns of "Happy Days," and in it there was both old and new music.

Coach told Danny to watch for the people who would set up a card table and collect money at the door. He said that when Danny paid for his ticket, they would give him three tokens for the juke box.

Soon the people with the card table were there and kids started coming through the door. Danny paid and got his three tokens. He didn't really know what songs he would spend his tokens on but figured one of the other kids would want to use them.

There were a lot of tables set around the edges of the gym and Danny went to one close to the jukebox and watched for his friends. He could see Coach Adams and his mom as they stood talking near the kitchen door. Mom looked really pretty tonight in a pink sweater and brown skirt. She looked even prettier when she looked at Coach Adams, and smiled and laughed like she was doing now. Danny breathed a sigh of contentment.

The first one of his friends to join him at the table was Polly. She looked especially nice and happy tonight too. When Gretchen came in dressed up, with a big smile on her face, Danny decided that girls must really like dances! David and Ray came over to the table and sat down with them and Danny was relieved to see that they looked just the same as ever, not all sparkly eyed like the girls. Maggie was the last of the Fun To Be One Club kids to come, and she looked the same too. *Good old Maggie; she's just like one of the guys!*

They knew that neither Kyleigh nor Scooter were going to be there. Even though their class, the one behind Danny's, was included in the dance, both sets of parents thought they were too young for dances.

Somebody started the music going with an old song, "Splish Splash." Danny thought it would be embarrassing to get out of the bathtub and find a party going on in his living room, and he couldn't imagine writing a song about it.

Nobody was on the gym floor dancing. Danny figured nobody wanted to be the first to get out there with everybody looking.

"Oh no!" Maggie groaned. "Look who's coming." Harold Sands was crossing the gym and heading right toward their table. "Seems like our group can't ever be alone these days."

Harold came up to the table and said to Maggie, "Would you like to dance?"

Maggie's face almost made Danny laugh. It froze. That was the only thing Danny could think of to describe the look she had. She just stared at Harold without saying a word.

Harold stood there looking at Maggie. Danny looked across the table at Maggie. Ray and David and Gretchen and Polly all looked at Maggie. Nobody said anything.

Finally, Polly's voice broke the uncomfortable silence.

"Maggie? Are you okay?"

Maggie turned to look at Polly. "Yes. Yes, I'm okay." She turned back to Harold. "I'm sorry, Harold. Thank you but I don't want to be the first one out there."

Harold just shrugged and turned away. A few minutes later he and a girl in Polly's class were out dancing on the gym floor. They were the only ones.

"Whew! That was weird. I couldn't believe he asked me to dance. I couldn't think of what to say." Maggie shook her head. "Thanks, Polly, for, well, for bringing me back from being frozen in the brain department!"

They all laughed.

Just then they heard some loud voices and saw that Leo and Eddie had walked in the gym and were talking about how stupid everything looked.

David said, "Then leave. Nobody wants you here anyway." But, of course, no one but his friends could hear him. They all nodded in agreement.

Before long, several girls were out on the floor dancing in a group.

"So, are you guys going to dance?" Ray asked the question of the whole table.

The rest shook their heads.

"Well, I am." Ray went across the floor to another table and led a pretty girl that none of the group knew out on the dance floor.

Danny knew someone was coming up behind him by the look on Maggie's face. He turned and saw Angela Wicker.

"Hi, Danny," she said shyly. "Are you ready for your first dance lesson?"

Danny could feel his face turn red. He didn't want to get out there in front of everybody but he didn't want to be rude either.

"Uh, I don't think so. Can't we just talk?"

Angela smiled and sat down at the table beside Danny. Danny noticed that as well as looking pretty, she smelled good.

Just then Gretchen came back to the table with a cup of punch. "This is really good; aren't you all going to have any refreshments?"

Maggie said, "I don't like punch. I might get some cookies. Anybody else going?"

"Not me," Angela answered. "Cookies and punch are both fattening."

"I'll get some cookies too." David got up to follow her and Danny saw Maggie roll her eyes at him, as she walked away.

Danny felt sorry for Angela. Anything she did made Maggie angry.

Gretchen gulped down her glass of punch and said she was going for a refill.

"So, are your mom and Coach Adams dating?" Angela smiled at Danny as she asked the question.

"I guess so. He goes to church with us now and takes us to lunch afterward. He comes over to the house sometimes. They haven't gone out, like to a movie or anything. But I think they are dating." Danny laughed. "I guess I'm just always there on their dates."

Gretchen came back with two cups of punch and Danny looked to see what happened to David and Maggie. They were by the refreshment table just standing there. Then he saw Coach bring out a pitcher of water and they filled two cups with water.

When they came back to the table, Gretchen said, "You got water? This punch is really good."

"I don't like two sweet things together," said Maggie. "I like milk and cookies or punch and chips."

"Yeah, me too," agreed David. "I never really thought about it but that's the way I am too. That's why I wanted water."

Gretchen had finished the first of the two cups she brought

back and was drinking the second. Her face looked flushed. "Well I think you're crazy! Whoa, it's getting hot in here, isn't it?"

Danny didn't feel hot but he looked at the others to see their reactions.

They were all shaking their heads.

Polly reached over and put her hand on Gretchen's forehead. "Are you sure you're not sick, Gretchen?"

Gretchen pushed her hand away. "No, not sick. Just thirsty." She stood up. "Going to get more punch."

They watched her walk over toward the punch bowl.

David stood up. "Look at her!"

Gretchen was walking in a wobbly kind of way, not in a straight line at all.

"Could somebody have put something in the punch?" David started after Gretchen just as she stumbled and almost fell.

Danny was shocked. Surely no one would have done that! But then he saw Coach Adams pick up the punch bowl and carry it back to the kitchen.

Chapter Nineteen

Unwelcome Letter

By lunchtime on Monday, all the middle school grade students had heard about Leo Baily being expelled from school for putting an alcoholic beverage in the punch at the dance on Friday night. Eddie Jackson had been suspended for the week but Leo would not be coming back. They were told there were other times that Leo had been in trouble over that year. Danny was not surprised.

But Danny felt kind of guilty for not praying for Leo. Maybe it would have helped after all. Like the preacher said Sunday during the sermon, God doesn't do anything in the earth unless some person prays for it. Danny resolved to begin praying for Leo. It was going to be a lot easier to pray for him when Leo wasn't right in front of him every day at school doing something mean to Danny or somebody else.

All the Fun To Be One Club members said that it was much nicer without Leo around but they also agreed with Danny that they should start praying for him.

"I wonder what Eddie Jackson will be like without Leo to tell him what to do?" David asked.

Before anyone could speculate on that question, Gretchen

interrupted.

"Thank you all for not teasing me about drinking all that punch Friday night."

"It wasn't your fault," Danny said quickly.

Gretchen laughed softly, "Well, it *was* my fault for drinking so much of it. But it wasn't my fault that alcohol was in it. I'm glad that they found out before I had any more."

"Yep, you sure were walking funny!" Maggie laughed. "But it wasn't funny at the time. We were just worried about you. Especially Polly. But then when we saw Coach Adams carry away the punch bowl while it was still half full, we realized what happened."

"I bet they won't have another dance any time soon." Ray looked sorry.

"Yeah, they will. Well, as soon as they would have anyway." Danny explained, "I heard my mom and the Coach talking. They are going to have an adult by the food table all the time. They are going to check backpacks and stuff when people come in."

Gretchen added, "Thank you for not telling anybody about me and the punch. Other people might not have been so nice. I saw Kyleigh in the girls restroom earlier and she said that the girl in her class that … well … that let them know something was wrong, has been teased all morning. I feel sorry for her."

Danny knew, also from hearing Mom and Coach talking, that the younger girl had started rolling on the floor and laughing hysterically. Some of the people at her table had gone to the chaperones and that was when they tasted the punch and found that it was spiked.

"I wonder why none of the kids tasted the alcohol," Danny asked.

"It was some kind that doesn't have much taste, but the adults were looking for it," David said. "That's kind of scary, isn't it? I mean, you didn't know, you didn't taste it, did you Gretchen?"

She shook her head. "No, not at all."

Danny thought it really was scary to think you could eat or

drink something dangerous without knowing it. He thought that was probably one of those things that they meant when Mom and Gramma and Grampa talked at Christmas about the world being safer when Mom was growing up, and even more safe when his grandparents were young.

Maggie was really in a good mood and Danny wondered if it was because Angela Wicker was not at school today.

≋

When the command came that afternoon, Danny restrained himself from looking triumphantly at Maggie. Since Angela wasn't even at school, it couldn't be her who was sending the signal. But as he was relaxing in that thought, he suddenly remembered the times when he had heard the command at his house, and nobody had been there with him.

The command again was "Hate" but the desire to be angry didn't even reach his emotions, just the word in his head let him know that the command had been given. As before, he began praying that everyone would experience God's love. It didn't even take very long today to stop the command from being sent and Danny wondered if Leo and Eddie being gone helped … they probably never even tried to fight a hate feeling, probably added to it.

That was something to think about!

≋

Because it was cold, the Fun To Be One Club met at Danny's apartment. When they had finished hot chocolate and microwave popcorn, Danny brought up the subject.

"I wonder if other people kind of, well, make the commands stronger by agreeing with them instead of fighting them." He told them about thinking that with Leo and Eddie gone, it was easier to stop the influence.

"And Angela," added Maggie. "She wasn't there either."

Danny didn't say anything.

Kyleigh said, "I'm glad that stuff doesn't happen in our class. At first I thought it was interesting and that I'd like to hear it. But

I've changed my mind. I'm glad my parents wouldn't let me go to that dance, too."

Scooter disagreed. He said he wished he could have seen what happened. The older kids were silent. They didn't want to tell even their friends that Gretchen had been a victim of Leo's actions.

Polly changed the subject. "Do we know any more about the Fun To Be One Club Camp this summer?"

David doubled his right hand into a fist and hit his left palm. "I forgot! I'm sorry. I had printed out the applications and was going to bring them today. I went off and left them on my desk at home."

"If I had a printer, we could do it here. I can look up anything but can't print ... yet!" Danny explained.

"Could we look it up now," asked Polly. "Or do you remember, David?"

"I remember some. It's the second week in July and we have to have recommendations from our pastors, and of course, our parents have to agree we can go, and pay the cost. There is a list of subjects we will be learning and stuff we'll be doing. And a list of things we should bring. I printed those off too."

"I want to see the stuff we'll be doing." Maggie turned to Danny. "Could we look it up on your computer?"

"Sure," he said. They all followed him to his room.

He was glad that he had cleaned up the junk off the floor last night and made his bed that morning. But he wished he had made the bed a little better ... or maybe a whole lot better. There were lumps, and the hem of the bedspread was pooled on the floor at the foot of the bed and a foot off the floor up by the pillows.

The kids all gathered around as Danny proudly brought up the FUN TO BE ONE CLUB site from his 'favorites' list.

There were pictures of the campground and all the kids liked the look of it as much as Danny did. The Clubhouse, or lodge, looked like a giant gingerbread house, and it sat close beside a small lake that had rowboats moored at a dock near its edge.

There were cottages set back in a wooded area on the other side of the Clubhouse and that was where the young campers would sleep.

There was also a softball field, a miniature golf course, and a craft pavilion as well as a swimming pool.

"Wow! I really hope we get to go," said Kyleigh. "But I don't know if my parents will let me." Danny remembered her fears about her parents' marriage and wondered if that had anything to do with her concern about camp. But then he realized that they hadn't let her go to the dance, so maybe it was just that they were really careful where she went.

David said, "My parents have already said I can go. Did Coach talk to your mom, Danny?"

"I don't think so. I don't know. We haven't talked about it … not me and Coach or Mom and me." He was a little more hopeful about the camp now that Coach and Mom were friends.

Friends. He hadn't really seen anything more than friends in their actions toward each other except that Mom looked really happy when Coach gave her a valentine card and she read what was inside of it. Coach looked at Mom really, well, really kind of gooey in Danny's opinion. But he had never seen them kiss or anything.

The group all decided that as soon as they got the application forms, they would go to their parents and ask.

"But won't we need to tell them about our Club?" Polly asked the question Danny had been thinking.

"I think so." David nodded. "I didn't tell my parents when I showed them the website. But they checked it out with our pastor."

"I don't know how to tell them," said Kyleigh in a quivery sort of voice.

Danny had an idea. "What if we invite all the parents together and Coach too since he's our sponsor? We'll tell them about the Club and ask about the camp at the same time."

"That's a great idea," said Ray. "They are much more likely to let us go if they see other parents letting their kids go."

They agreed to have Danny talk to Coach Adams about when and where. They closed with prayer, and the Fun To Be One Club meeting broke up.

Danny realized after the others left that they never had talked about whether who was in the classroom would make a difference in the strength of a command.

≈≈≈

Mom had the mail in her hand when she came home from work. That was usually Danny's job but with the kids coming over, he forgot all about it that afternoon.

"Sorry about the mail, Mom."

"No big deal. I don't know why I even stopped to unlock the box. But I'm glad I did." She put the mail on the counter and laid the sack on the kitchen table. Danny took out the Styrofoam containers. Tonight was hot roast beef sandwiches with mashed potatoes and gravy.

Danny told Mom about Leo being expelled and she nodded. She said they heard about it in the kitchen. Coach Adams had stopped by the restaurant later on and told her that Leo's parents were sending him to a boarding school.

The meal was good and Danny ate every bite. Mom looked tired and he picked up both of their containers, threw them away, and put the forks and knives in the sink, rinsing them off before he left them.

"Danny."

He turned around. Mom was smiling at him. "You are a really good boy and I am very proud of you."

He could feel his face getting red. At first he didn't say anything because he didn't know what to say.

After a minute, he said, "Thank you. I'm proud of you too!"

She asked, "Have you had your shower?"

"No, after the kids left, I did homework and then watched TV for a while."

"Well you go ahead because when you finish I want to soak

for a long time in a hot tub. I am really tired and achy tonight."

"Okay!" He got his sleep pants and headed to the bathroom.

When Danny got out of the shower, he yelled toward the living room, "Okay, I'm through. You can have the bathroom."

He had been in his room a few minutes when he realized that Mom hadn't passed by on her way to take a bath. She had never answered him. Maybe she hadn't heard.

She wasn't in the living room so he went back into the kitchen. Mom was sitting at the table with the pile of mail in front of her. She was staring at a letter in her hand.

Danny could tell by the look on her face that something was very wrong.

"Mom, what?" He put his hand on her shoulder and she immediately turned the letter upside down.

"Mom?"

She still didn't answer.

"Mom, is something wrong with Gramma or Grampa?"

She shook her head. He realized that if there had been something wrong with his grandparents, they would have gotten a phone call, not a letter. He saw the envelope sitting off to the side and looked at the return address. She snatched at it but not before Danny had seen the name Alcorn in the upper left hand corner.

Before she even said anything, he knew.

Mom drew a deep breath and said, "Sit down, Son."

Danny pulled out a chair across the table from her and sat.

"It's from your father, Danny. He wants to come and visit. He wants to see you."

Danny's eyes narrowed. "Well I don't want to see him!"

"Danny, he is your father."

"No, he's not. I don't have a father. Except God." Danny knew he was talking too loud and even sounded like he was mad at Mom but he couldn't help it.

She looked at him and her eyes were very sad. "Yes, Danny. You do have a father, an earthly one. I was afraid this day might come."

Danny didn't say anything.

"Oh, Danny. I guess I shouldn't feel like that. I should be happy that he has quit drinking and I am. I guess it's just, well, for so many years I hoped for that, prayed for it. Then I gave up. I've watched so many other single moms have to share their children on holidays. It's selfish of me but I've loved having you all to myself. I mean, it would have been nice to have help with money and discipline and all but ..."

Danny almost exploded. "WE DON'T NEED HIM!"

"No," she agreed. "We don't need him, but it sounds like he needs us, well, he needs you." She picked up the letter. "He says he tracked us down from my last job in the city. He is going to be coming here – to the city – this spring on a business trip. He wants to meet his son."

"Do I have to?" Danny still felt angry but he also felt a sense of doom, like it was going to happen whether he wanted it to or not.

She nodded. "I think so."

"That's not fair! He never even wrote. He never helped you. He never cared about either one of us. How can he just come back like he ... like he owned us or something?"

"It's not like that, Son. We're divorced and he is behind thousands of dollars in child support. It's really to his advantage to stay missing. I could have him arrested for non–support and he knows it." She pointed at the letter. "But he says he wants to talk to me about that too. He says he is sorry."

Danny was gritting his teeth and didn't respond.

"He must want to see you a lot." Mom was trying to encourage him, Danny could tell.

"Well, I don't want to see him!" Danny repeated his initial reaction.

Just then the phone rang.

Chapter Twenty

Go Away

Danny was so quiet at school the next day that his friends kept trying to find out what was wrong. He just shook his head. He didn't want to talk about … *him*!

He wouldn't even talk to his mom anymore last night about it. When Mom went to answer the phone, Danny went to his room and crawled into bed. In a few minutes, Mom knocked on his door but he said, "Go away." He knew that he shouldn't be rude to his mother, but he just couldn't help it.

"Danny, Jerry … Coach Adams wants to talk to you."

"No."

"Please, Danny."

"No, I don't want to talk to anybody."

After she left Danny got up, brushed a tear away, and picked up his Bible. But when he opened it, it seemed like all the words just ran together. He closed it and got on his knees. "God I know you are there, even if I can't feel you. I don't want to see *him*. Please don't make me. Amen."

Then he turned off the light and got back in bed. After a long time Danny heard someone knock on the front door and then heard voices in the living room and he knew that Coach Adams had come over, and he and Mom were talking.

They were talking too low for Danny to hear what they were saying and he told himself he didn't want to hear anyway.

He didn't want to admit even to himself that he was scared. But he was. *What if he comes back and Mom wants to marry him again? We'll have to move away to be where he lives. I'll lose my friends. What if he starts drinking again? And yelling and ... hitting?*

"Please, God, please." Danny fell asleep with the pillow over his face.

When the command "hate" came after lunch the next day, Danny dove into it as if it were a swimming pool and it felt good at first.

Danny saw a picture in his mind of the man as he remembered him. Mostly it was just the cigar smell and yelling and thick dark eyebrows. The man was really little and Danny was really big. Danny kicked him in the head, just like in some of the movies he used to watch, until blood came out the man's mouth. Danny was glad.

Suddenly Jesus was there in the scene in Danny's mind. Jesus walked into the man. Not bumped into the man but walked into him, and Jesus and the man were one and Danny was kicking Jesus in the head.

Danny remembered something he read one night in the Bible, something Jesus said, "As you do to the least of these, you do it to me." Suddenly the scene disappeared and Danny put his head down on the desk. *I'm sorry. I'm sorry, Lord. Help me not hate. Even him!*

Danny felt someone put an arm around him. He knew if he looked up, he wouldn't see anybody. He had felt that arm before.

When he lifted his head from the desk, Danny saw Maggie smile and give him a thumbs-up. He figured that she thought he had been helping her and the others fight the hate for their classmates. He knew they had fought it for him.

On his way home from school that day, Danny was joined by Harold Sands. At first, the two boys just walked along in silence. Danny wished Harold would go away.

Finally the other boy spoke. "Thank you for what you did in the restroom that day. Leo's gone now, but he never did bother me again after you stopped him. He'd been taking all my money for a long time, ever since school started this year."

Danny was surprised. "He took mine too for a while. I quit bringing snacks or money with me and he stopped bothering me."

"I'm glad he got expelled."

"Me too," agreed Danny. "Maybe they can help him in that private school."

Harold stopped walking. Danny turned around to see the other boy staring at him.

"What?"

"You are really strange, man. I mean, Leo was as mean to you as to me – and you hope that they help him?"

"Well, yeah. I mean, isn't that what the Bible says ... pray for your enemies and do good to the ones who are mean to you?"

"Yeah, but ..."

Danny went on. "I admit that I couldn't pray for Leo when he was here; it's easier when I don't have to see him everyday."

Harold said, "I don't pray for anybody."

"I thought you went to church."

"Well, yeah. But ..." Harold stopped as if he didn't know what to say about church.

"But you don't really know Jesus, right?" Danny couldn't believe that he was saying that. His heart was pounding. *Me? The one who makes up pictures in his mind of kicking his own father in the head?*

Harold shook his head. "I'm not sure I really believe in Jesus."

"I'm sorry," said Danny.

"What do you mean?" The old sneer came back in Harold's voice. "Afraid I am going to hell?"

Danny thought a minute. "Well, that too. But mostly I was

thinking how awful it would be not to know Him and how much He loves you."

Before he thought it out, he was telling Harold about his father and how he left them when Danny was really young, and about the letter, and about giving into the hate command, and about seeing Jesus walk into the picture, and about feeling Jesus put his arm around him. *Harold? Telling Harold all that stuff? Harold Sands? Now he'd really have something to make fun of Danny about.*

But to his great shock, when Danny looked over at the other boy, he saw Harold wiping away a tear that was straying down his cheek. They were at the place on the street where they needed to go separate ways but Danny surprised himself again by saying, "Would you like to come to my place and talk?"

Harold nodded.

By the time the two boys had let themselves into the apartment, Harold wasn't crying.

Danny said, "You can call your mom and let her know where you are." He pointed to the phone.

Harold shook his head. "No, she's not home anyway. She never knows where I am. It doesn't matter."

Danny was shocked. His own mom always insisted on knowing where he was every minute. But he didn't say anything.

The boys made peanut butter and jelly sandwiches, each got a glass of milk and sat down at the kitchen table.

They talked about Leo and the Valentine dance but they seemed to be steering away from the subject of Jesus. Danny didn't know how to bring it up again.

When Danny had rinsed the rest of the milk from the glasses, they went into his room and he showed Harold his computer.

"That's cool," the other boy said. Danny waited to hear how much better Harold's computer was, but it didn't happen.

"I wish I had a printer," Danny admitted.

"Yeah, a printer is cool. I got one when I got the computer." But Harold seemed to stop himself before the bragging began.

"Maybe you'll get one soon."

"I think I'm going to ask for one for my birthday. I think you can get them without too much money." Danny's birthday was in March and he hoped maybe Mom, Gramma and Grampa could all go in together and get it for him.

Danny kept thinking that he needed to talk about Jesus some more … get Harold to ask Jesus into his heart and all that but he couldn't seem to think of the right words.

When the other boy left, they still had not mentioned Him.

Danny was surprised when a knock came on the door just a few minutes after Harold left. He thought he must be coming back and Danny breathed a quick prayer before he answered the door. "Lord, help me say what you want me to say."

But when he opened the door, it wasn't Harold. Coach Adams was standing there. "Danny, may I come in?"

Danny nodded and stood back to let Coach enter.

Coach waited until Danny invited him to sit down.

"Sir, I am sorry about last night, that I wouldn't talk to you. I just, well, I just needed to think about it. I haven't thought about *him* in a long time. I just tried to pretend that he wasn't real, I think."

"I understand, Danny. I really do. I wasn't mad that you wouldn't talk to me. I just prayed for you, that you would know what is best."

Danny shook his head. "I was really, really mad." He described what had happened that afternoon in the classroom. "Now all the hate is gone. I still don't want to see him and I don't know why he wants to see me."

Coach Adams smiled. "I understand why he wants to see you; you're his son. He will be proud of you."

Danny shook his head. He didn't want to tell Coach his biggest fear … that Mom would want to be married to him again.

"Maybe he needs to ask your forgiveness, Danny. I read the letter he sent to your mom and it seems like he is really sorry for the way he treated you both, when he lived with you and after the divorce."

"I forgive him. Can't I just write a letter back saying I forgive him?"

Coach smiled. "What do you think?"

Danny breathed a deep sigh. "I think Jesus wants me to meet him for some reason."

Coach nodded.

"Oh, I did an awful thing today." Danny told him about the time spent with Harold and how he never could get back around to getting Harold to ask Jesus into his life.

"Danny, I don't think you did an awful thing at all. Didn't you say you were surprised at what all you said when you were walking?"

Danny nodded.

"Well, you were being obedient to the Holy Spirit, weren't you, even if you were uncomfortable doing it?"

Danny nodded again.

"So, don't you think that if the Holy Spirit wanted you to say more about that later, He would have let you know?"

Relief flooded Danny. "But why wouldn't He want me to do that?"

"There is such a thing as timing, Son. A lot of Christians drive people farther away from God by pushing them too soon. Remember the parable Jesus told about the sower sowing the Word of God?"

"Yes, Sir."

"That first seed fell on hard ground and was stolen away by the enemy. I think that is a picture of what happens when the ground isn't prepared … and by that I mean that prayer and acts of love get the ground of human hearts ready to accept the new life Jesus brings. That is the responsibility of the Body of Christ, of Christians." Danny thought about that for a minute and then nodded. "That makes sense. I have been praying for Harold. I guess today God gave me a chance to do an act of love by asking him over."

"Yes, exactly! You'll know when God wants you to do something else."

Danny told Coach how Harold said it didn't matter where he was, that he didn't need to let his mom know.

"Want to pray about that?"

"Yeah, please."

Coach took Danny's hand and led them in prayer. "Father, I want to thank you for Danny and we hold up the time when he will meet his father. Lord, we ask you to prepare Danny and his mom and his dad for that meeting and pray your will be done for them all. Lord, we hold up Harold Sands. He needs you. He needs his family to let him know they care about him too. We agree with you for Harold and the life you have planned for him. Help him discover it and walk in it. We claim Harold and his entire family for the Kingdom of God in the name of Jesus. Amen."

When Mom came in from work that night, Danny kissed her and said, "Let's write a letter to my father."

And they did.

Chapter Twenty-One

Confession

Danny was home alone when the phone call came, and he heard his father's voice for the first time in nine years.

"Danny?"

"Yes?"

"This is your dad. I was so glad when I got the letter from you and your mom." The strange voice talked fast, like he was afraid Danny might hang up. "Thank you for writing me back. I know it's a shock to hear from me after all these years, and you're probably very angry at me. But I hope I can make it up to you and we can have a father and son relationship in the future."

Danny didn't know what to say. He didn't feel hate for his father any more but he didn't feel anything else either. So he just asked, "When are you coming here?"

"Well, it will be about the time of your birthday – that week I'll be working in the city. I thought if you didn't already have plans, maybe I could come and see you that Saturday?"

Danny didn't have plans but he wished he did. This man was a stranger.

"You'll have to ask Mom." He knew his voice didn't sound

very friendly but he couldn't make himself sound friendly when he didn't feel it.

"Is she there?"

"No, she'll be in around eight tonight."

"Okay, Son, I'll call back then. Thank you again."

"Okay."

"Bye, Danny."

"Bye."

When Danny hung up the phone, he just stood there looking at it for a few minutes. *Son. He called me son. That feels weird. When Coach calls me son it feels good.* Danny sighed.

Coach! He never asked Coach when and how they could set it up to talk to the parents about camp. Polly'd asked him twice now but so much had been going on that he kept forgetting. Danny picked up the phone again and called Coach Adam's house. When there was no answer, he left a message on the answer machine.

"Hi, it's Danny. I need to talk to you about the Fun To Be One Club so could I stop by your office tomorrow? Unless you want to call me back before Mom gets home. But I think we're all going to tell our parents about it. That's what I want to talk to you about. Okay. Bye."

Danny thought the message probably sounded dumb but at least Coach would know what he wanted to talk about, sort of.

≈≈≈

They all arrived at the Clubhouse at different times and Danny was the last one there. Coach called him back last night before Mom got home but he still stopped by the office after school because they spent most of the phone call talking about the upcoming visit with Danny's dad. Coach had prayed with him about it again.

When they were all settled on their cushions, Maggie brought up the parents meeting. "Did you finally ask Coach Adams? What did he say?"

"He said he thought it was good that we were going to tell our parents. He thought we should all go ahead and tell them about our club. After that tell them about the camp and that there is a meeting set up for all the parents to get together and talk. He said it would be nice to have a meeting on a Sunday afternoon and we can have it at his house this Sunday if we want to."

"That's great!" David looked very happy about the solution. "My parents have already checked the camp out so they will help talk to them about it."

They all agreed to go ahead and tell their parents that night and find out if everybody could meet on Sunday. They prayed and made Jesus Lord over the meeting and asked God to help their parents see that The Fun To Be One Club is a good thing.

"Now!" said Polly. "What is going on in your class? You haven't mentioned the commands in a long time."

"That's because nothing has happened," David answered her.

"It just quit?" Scooter asked.

"It just quit," said Gretchen.

"That's strange." Polly shook her head.

"Well, wasn't that what our goal was? To put a stop to it?" David looked around at the group.

Suddenly Danny laughed. "I think we wanted more than that really, we wanted to be detectives and find out who was doing it. But I guess God just wanted us to pray for the person and get them to quit doing it. We did, and they did."

Maggie frowned. "Yeah, I guess. But I sure would like to know who it was ... who *she* was." She looked knowingly at Danny.

Danny still did not believe that Angela Wicker was the one. Angela had retreated again behind her books and didn't join the group any more at the lunch table but she didn't sneer at everybody any more either.

Kyleigh spoke up with her soft, gentle voice. "Can I talk about something else?"

"Of course," David said. "You can talk about anything you want to."

"I just wanted to say that God is very good and he answers a lot of kinds of prayers." She looked over at Danny. "Danny knows, because one day he came back and I was still here and I was crying. I was afraid my parents were going to get a divorce and I prayed and prayed and finally gave up. I thought God didn't listen. But Danny told me that I just couldn't see what God was doing. He was right." Her smile made them all feel happy along with her. "Everything is really good now. They are going to counseling and seem really happy together."

"That's great, Kyleigh!" Polly reached over and hugged the younger girl.

"Okay!" Danny blurted out. "I've got something I want you all to pray about."

They turned their attention to him.

He told them about the letter from his father. How his parents talked last night and agreed for the three of them to meet. The meeting would be the day before Easter.

"Are you excited about meeting your dad?" Ray really sounded interested.

"No," said Danny. "That's why I need you all to pray. I don't want to meet him at all." Then he admitted what happened the last time the hate command had come, and how he had given into it. "But ever since then I haven't hated him. What's strange is that ever since then there haven't been any more commands. I think you all prayed Jesus into everybody's hate, even the one who sent it!"

"I hope so!" David said with a sigh.

Danny had been the last member of the Fun To Be One Club to arrive that afternoon and he was the last one to leave. He wanted to stay and pray alone.

He had been just sitting on his cushion in the quiet for about 15 minutes when he was startled by the sound of the door opening. He opened his eyes and looked up just as Harold Sands looked in. The two just stared at each other for several seconds. Then Harold said, "I thought everybody left."

"You've been spying on us?"

The other boy's face turned red. He just nodded.

"Well, come on in. Have you been here before?"

Harold entered and closed the door behind him. "No, this is the first time. I just found out where you were going last week. I mean, you used to go to your place but last week I saw you all heading this way and I followed Maggie."

"Were you listening to what we said?"

Harold shook his head. "No, I promise. I just saw where you went and thought that the next time I'd come in to see the inside. And I did." He looked around.

Danny said, "Well sit down. Here, take my cushion. I'll use Maggie's; she won't mind." He laughed as he thought of his own first time inside the Clubhouse.

Harold sat down as Danny got out the other cushion.

"Danny, I've been thinking about what you said that day I went home with you. You know, about knowing Jesus."

Danny nodded.

"I can tell you really do know him, like he's alive and real. But I don't know how to get to know him."

Here it is! Coach was right. Danny smiled. "It's real easy, Harold. It's easy because He *is* alive and He wants us to know him. So he does all the work; we just ask him." Danny looked straight into Harold's eyes. "Do you believe that Jesus really was the Son of God?"

Harold said, "Sure."

"Do you believe he died because of our sins?"

"Yeah. I learned all that at church"

"Then just thank him for doing it and ask him to come in and live in your heart and mind."

There was silence. Then Harold said, "You mean now?"

"Yeah, why not?"

"Okay." Harold bowed his head. Then he looked up. "This feels really weird. I don't think I can do it."

"Why not?"

"Well, there's some stuff I did that's really bad. I don't think

Jesus would want to live in my heart and mind."

"Yeah, he would. I promise. I've done some really bad stuff too, even after he came to live there. But he stays anyway. He washes the bad stuff away."

"Really?"

"Really. He really loves us, Harold. He really loves you and he forgives all the bad stuff."

"Okay." Harold bowed his head again. Again he raised it. "I don't think I can do it until I tell you about it."

Danny didn't want to hear bad stuff Harold Sands had done but if this was part of how God wanted to use him to help his classmate he would do it.

"Okay."

"It was me who did the spells in class."

Later Danny thought that it was a good thing he was sitting down because Harold's confession was such a shock that his knees might have buckled if he had been standing.

"No way!"

"Yeah, it was me. I read those wizard books over the summer and then went and got some on witchcraft too. I thought it would be fun to make people do stuff. So I tried it the first day of school. It worked … on most people. I always pretended to go to sleep too so if anybody figured it out, that it was a spell, I mean, then they wouldn't suspect me."

"So you were the one who really made Leo hit me with the basketball and you said 'she' to throw me off the track."

Harold grinned a sickly, weak kind of smile. "Well, no, not exactly. That was just an accident – or maybe Leo did it on purpose. I just said that to make you think that the person who did the spells was more powerful than they, I, really was."

"But what about you … you got hit too. Did you make the ball hit your own head?"

This time Harold actually blushed. "I paid Eddie to throw the ball at me. When Coach went over to talk to Leo and sent Eddie away, I gave him a dollar and told him to throw it when I was talking to you. It didn't really knock me out. I just pretended. I really couldn't do anything but send out those thoughts in the classroom."

"But what about the mice? You controlled the mice."

Harold shook his head vigorously. "I brought those mice in a cage and left them in a cupboard at the back of the room until after lunch. At lunch time I sneaked back in the room and put some peanut butter in Maggie's desk ... I brushed up against her when she came back in the room and put peanut butter on her jeans."

"But what about the map? You caused that to fly up?"

"Nope. I saw you all look at each other and knew you thought it was a spell but it wasn't. I laughed over that. You all thought there was really some powerful wizard in the room. Or witch."

Danny sat there just shaking his head.

"So none of it was real?"

"The spells were real. That's scary. To think that we can do that, I mean. To think that we can use our minds to make other people feel things. I thought it was fun at first and it made me feel important. But then it didn't seem funny any more. You were so nice to me and I felt, well I felt ashamed of myself."

Danny nodded. "I can understand that. Well, what about that! The others ... oh, I guess you don't want me to tell them." Then as an afterthought, he added, "Did you know that we were praying against your spells?"

"I knew something was fighting them. That day that you told me that you all got together and prayed and talked about the Bible, I started thinking maybe it was you, all of you."

"So ... can I tell them it was you?"

"I wish you wouldn't," Harold had a pleading look in his eyes and Danny understood. He wouldn't want everybody to know it if he had been the one giving the commands. So he nodded.

"That's not the really important thing anyway. The important thing is to ask Jesus to forgive you for, well, for messing around with witchcraft."

"Okay." Harold bowed his head again. This time, his head stayed bowed.

"Dear God, I'm sorry I did that witchcraft stuff. I know it's wrong. Will you forgive me? God, I do believe that Jesus died for me. I should die because of all the bad stuff I've done but Jesus died instead of me. Jesus, I thank you for dying for me. Will you please come and live with me? Danny says you will live in my heart and mind if I ask you to. So I am asking now. Uh … Amen."

Danny added to the prayer. "Father, thank you for Harold wanting Jesus to come and live in him. I ask you to wipe away all the witchcraft stuff out of him just like you wiped away all the hate stuff out of me. In Jesus' Name, Amen."

He looked up and smiled at the other boy. Harold was smiling back at him.

They both nodded.

HE was present and they knew it.

Chapter Twenty-Two

Parents Meeting

Only Danny's mom and Maggie's parents could meet that
Sunday afternoon so the "Fun To Be One Club with Parents"
meeting was postponed for two weeks.

Danny was getting more and more uncomfortable about being
the only one who knew Harold's secret. It didn't seem fair that the
others were still wondering and he knew the answer. It broke the
rule about keeping secrets, but he didn't want to betray a
confidence either. Besides being uncomfortable around the other
kids, he felt uncomfortable around Coach too. Whenever Mom
wasn't around, Coach Adams asked him about the commands, if
they were still not happening. Danny always just nodded and
changed the subject.

Coach Adams now went to church with them every Sunday
and then they either went out to eat or back to their apartment.
Mom said she got enough of restaurant food and thought Coach
and Danny didn't have enough home cooking either. So she
usually cooked something on Saturday that they could warm up
on Sunday afternoon.

Danny was glad that they were spending time together. It

seemed like time was building a wall between him and the nightmare of his mom getting married to his father again. *Nightmare!*

Danny got chill bumps all over when he remembered his nightmare at the first of the school year. *The light form shimmered brightly and gathered itself together in a brilliant burst of green—shattering splendor and there before him stood a man. The man laughed "Don't worry, my son … I will never leave you."*

No man had ever called Danny "my son" and though the presence of the man was a little frightening, Danny liked the way the man made him feel like he belonged to him.

The man held out his arms and said, "Come to me. Come to me of your own free will and you will be mine forever and you will never again feel alone and I will let no one bully you. I will be your father forever and you will be my son."

Could that dream have been a warning about his father? Danny remembered that he had wanted to run into the man's arms but something stopped him. The second nightmare was worse.

This time he said nothing but held out his arms. Danny wanted to run into them for protection but suddenly he noticed that the man's lips were bright red, like a vampire.

Oh, no! A horrible thought occurred to Danny. He didn't want to see his real father but in the nightmare, he had wanted to go to the man for protection. In real life, it was Coach he ran to for protection. Could his dream have been telling him that Coach Adams was really bad, or at least bad for Mom and him? Maybe it was God's plan that his parents get married again. Didn't the Bible say that God hates divorce?

Danny fell to his knees and put his head on the couch. "God, please help me! I don't know what's going on. All of a sudden nothing seems right. Mostly I am scared about my father coming here. I don't want Coach Adams to be wrong for us, for Mom and me. God, I hate having secrets from the other kids in the Club, and from Coach. I can't do anything about any of it, but you can. Please help me! In Jesus' Name, Amen."

Danny didn't get up right away but kept kneeling with his head on the couch cushion. He remembered how God had shown him that God wanted to make him, Danny, like Jesus. He suddenly realized that's why God wanted His people to pray in Jesus' Name. Pray just like they were Jesus. Danny lifted up his head. Of course, God would answer his prayer. He could relax. God was going to take care of it.

≋

They were all seated on their cushions at the Clubhouse.

"How did it go with your parents?" David looked around the group, one face at a time.

"Mine were fine with it," said Maggie. "They think it's a good thing and are looking forward to meeting with all your parents."

Ray grimaced. "Mine were kind of suspicious. But they'll be there."

Polly reported, "Mine will be there too, but I don't know what they thought. They didn't say anything else, just that they would be there. I think they are waiting to see what everybody else says."

Scooter said, "My parents are coming but they were mad that I had been … well not lying exactly … but when I said I had a meeting after school they thought it was at the school." He paused a minute. "I knew they thought that. But they are coming! That's the main thing."

Danny said, "Mom was fine with it."

"My parents were like Scooter's. They were mad that I hadn't been honest with them about the meetings. But they are coming." Gretchen nodded.

David's gaze came to rest on Kyleigh.

"They are coming too. They didn't mind us getting together but they were kind of like yours," she looked over at Gretchen and Scooter. "They were, well, not mad, but more scared that I had been somewhere they didn't know about. I told them about the camp and they shook their heads and looked at each other. But, like Gretchen said … they're coming!"

David said, "Mine too! They'd already said it was okay about the camp."

He nodded. "So, what now?"

Maggie spoke up. "It's weird. Now that we aren't fighting the commands anymore, it feels strange. Now that we're not a secret club – I mean our parents know – it's even stranger."

Ray agreed. "It's not as much fun. I guess that's bad, part of original sin or something, that it's more fun to be doing something sneaky?"

David said, "When you put it that way, it does seem awful. But you're right. It did seem more fun when it was a secret."

Gretchen added, "I am glad that the commands are gone but you're right about that too. That was kind of fun too – fighting them and winning, I mean."

David laughed. "We're a mess, aren't we? We miss witchcraft and being sneaky?"

"I guess she just got tired of giving the commands." Maggie looked triumphant. "Because we won every time! She just gave up trying."

"Maggie, you don't know that it was a girl." Danny reminded her.

"Oh, yes I do!" She glared at Danny.

"No you don't!" He heard his voice getting louder and knew he should shut up, but he didn't. "You don't know what you're talking about!"

"Oh, yes I do," Maggie repeated. "You just don't want to believe it's your girlfriend!" She sneered at Danny.

"I told you I don't have or even want a girlfriend! It's not Angela Wicker that was giving the commands. It was a boy, not a girl!"

The others had been watching the exchange with dismay on their faces but the dismay turned to shock at Danny's last words.

Uh-oh. I've had it now!

David said sternly, "Danny? You know who was doing it?"

Danny dropped his head. "I …"

Suddenly he couldn't stand it. It seemed like his whole life was falling apart. His friends would never forgive him for not telling, for keeping secrets. What did it matter anyway? His father would probably make them move away and he wouldn't have any friends anymore anyway. Danny got up and, without even putting his cushion away, he ran out the door.

The last thing he heard was Gretchen's voice asking, "Was it him? Was Danny the one giving the commands?"

Danny ran all the way home. He went to the kitchen, got out a package of cookies, and turned on the television to a cartoon show he used to watch.

The cookies were hard to swallow but he was trying to pretend that nothing was wrong, that he wasn't hurt by Gretchen's question, when someone knocked on the apartment door. He just ignored it and went on watching TV.

"Danny, I know you're in there. I saw you go home."

No! Not Harold Sands ...

"Please, Danny, I need to talk to you."

Danny sighed but he got up, wiping away the crumbs from his shirt and the tears from his cheeks.

When he let Harold in, the other boy just stood there instead of sitting down.

"I just wanted to say that I'm sorry. I mean for asking you not to tell the others that it was me doing the spells. It's okay. You can tell them. I deserve it."

It was the word deserve that got to Danny. He sighed. "We all deserve a lot of bad things, Harold. But God doesn't work that way. He doesn't give us what we deserve. He only gives us good things." *Aren't you a fine one to be talking about how nice God is? Right in the middle of not trusting Him yourself!*

"Okay ... so He doesn't punish but I know He wants me to confess to them too, that it was me. Especially I need to tell Maggie and ask her to forgive me."

Danny thought about that for a minute. Then he nodded. "Okay, let's go."

≈≈≈

Everything was okay again ... well, almost everything. There was still the father thing to go through but Danny could handle that better now that everything was okay between him and his friends. The kids were still there when he and Harold got to the Fun To Be One Clubhouse. They looked shocked when Harold came in with Danny but soon were welcoming him as a new part of their family in Christ Jesus.

Harold asked forgiveness for the witchcraft thing and for spying on them.

They forgave him for everything.

When he turned to leave, David looked around at everyone with a question in his eyes. Danny understood what he was asking and nodded. Everyone else must have understood too because they nodded also.

David got up and put his hand on Harold's shoulder. "Harold, it seems that the King has made you one of us. Do you want to stay?"

The joy that flooded the boy's face made him look like a new person. Danny thought, "He is a new person! Just like me."

When Harold sat back down Maggie explained about the pillows, David told him about the Camp, and Danny told him about the meeting at Coach's house. Harold wasn't sure how his mom would take it all.

"She's not very religious," he said.

≈≈≈

That Sunday afternoon at 3 o'clock, all the parents met at Coach's house. Danny and his mom had gone there right after church with Coach; it was the first time they'd been to his house. Mom baked some cookies the night before to have at the meeting but they picked up fried chicken dinners after church and ate lunch around the table in Coach Adam's kitchen. Then Mom made coffee and set out things for tea while the Coach and Danny arranged extra chairs in the living room; Coach had borrowed folding chairs from the school.

Danny thought Coach's house was pretty neat. There were pictures and models of clipper ships in the living room. There were sports trophies in a cabinet in the hallway.

When the last family arrived, Coach Adams asked everyone to bow their head while he opened the meeting with prayer.

"Lord, we are gathered here in your name and ask you to open the eyes of our understanding. Increase your love and life in our hearts so that we may see your plan in the lives of these young people, so we can help and not hinder what you want to do to train them and bring them into the future you have planned."

Then he began talking, looking at each parent in turn straight in the eyes as he spoke.

"At the end of last school year, several of your children came to me and asked me to be a sponsor for them in a Christian group they had formed. The Fun To Be One Club. I was hesitant because they didn't want any other adults to know about it, at that time. I prayed but felt that the Lord wanted me to help them, and that He would handle the secrecy matter in His own time and way.

"Those original members – David, Maggie, Ray, and Gretchen were joined by Kyleigh, Scooter, and Polly by the end of the summer and then Danny came to be a part of them last fall. Just recently, Harold was added to their number." At this, he smiled at the newest member.

"They found out the name they chose was very appropriate because there was a national ministry organization by the same name, dedicated to the same purpose: bonding together members of the Body of Christ from all different denominations in order to help each other and combat evil in our present society.

"They also discovered there's a Fun To Be One Club summer camp where people from all over the United States come together with their own age group to learn more about the Christian walk and pray and just have good clean fun. Some sports, horse back riding, swimming, lessons in those things for those who need them. They have a Nurse Practitioner on the grounds at all times. For what it's worth, I think it's a great organization."

He then asked. "Any questions? Comments?"

Danny looked around at everybody's parents.

David's father was the first to speak. "I checked out the organization and talked to the national Director. I was very impressed and plan to let David go this summer."

"How much does it cost?" Polly's mother twisted her hair as she asked the question.

David's dad explained the cost and said, "I know it seems kind of high but the Director said there are scholarships. Some people donate money for kids who can't afford it to go to camp. When you send in the application, you state how much you can pay, if any."

When he said that, Danny felt excitement stirring inside. He had been afraid that everyone was going to get to go but him, because Mom wouldn't be able to afford it. But he should have known that God would have another plan!

Danny saw Polly's parents look at each other and nod.

Ray's father said, "I asked our pastor and he seemed to think there was no harm in it. He looked it up and it is inter–racial as well as inter–denominational."

"Transdenominational," Scooter blurted out. All the kids except Harold laughed. Danny remembered how proud Scooter was for learning that word.

Ray's father smiled, "Transdenominational, then." He looked around at the others. "Maybe transracial too, huh?"

Danny looked around the group and realized that they *were* transracial. There was Polly with her Native American heritage, Gretchen whose mother was from the Philippines, and Ray's family who were African American.

Scooter's mom said, "I think we will send our son too. It sounds like a good experience."

Maggie's dad said, "Count Maggie in. We got the application and it looked legitimate but we wanted to meet all of you before making a decision." Beside him, his wife nodded.

Kyleigh's father spoke up. "We are still not happy about the dishonesty concerning the meetings. I want to make sure that Clubhouse – chicken coop – is safe."

Kyleigh looked around at the other kids apologetically. But Danny thought it was a good idea.

"We came here ready to say no, but after hearing what you have to say," Kyleigh's dad looked pointedly at Coach Adams and David's father, "I think we will do some investigating on our own and pray about it before making a decision."

Danny loved the glow on Kyleigh's face and noticed that it got even brighter when her father reached over and took her mother's hand after he finished speaking.

But then the cold feeling that had been in his stomach for the last month made itself felt. He was glad Kyleigh's parents were okay, but he didn't want his own parents to get back together.

When they left the meeting, the parents were all acting friendly to each other and it was settled that David, Maggie, Danny, Ray, Polly, Scooter, and Harold were going to camp. Gretchen's parents, like Kyleigh's were going to make a decision later.

The Fun To Be One Club kids all smiled at each other. They knew that God would work it out where the two girls would be included in their summer fun.

Chapter Twenty-Three

New Beginnings

Danny called for a special meeting of the Fun To Be One Club on Good Friday. They were all there except Kyleigh who went to Mass with her parents.

"I'm really scared," Danny confessed to his friends. "I don't want to meet my father. I need you to pray for me."

Polly suggested that they all make a circle around Danny. He could feel warmth surrounding him as they moved into place. He didn't think that the warmth was all body heat. It was love.

Maggie spoke first, "Father, you are the best father, the one who never leaves us and who is always there. Help Danny not be afraid. Please."

Scooter said, "God, make Danny have fun with his dad."

Gretchen laughed softly. "Yes, Lord, give Danny a good surprise and let this be fun for him."

Danny couldn't imagine that happening but he didn't want to hurt Scooter's or Gretchen's feelings by saying, "No way!"

Harold's voice was a little shaky and Danny figured it was because it was the first time he had prayed out loud in front of them. "God, I thank you for Danny. He is a good friend ... to you and to us. Help his father see how good he is and be nice to him. Amen."

Ray added, "Help Danny see the good in his father too."

Yeah, right!

Polly said, "Father, we ask you to cause Danny's dad to know you ..." She paused. "Unless he already does."

David simply said, "Amen."

"That was strange," Polly said. "Danny, I think your dad is a Christian."

That was a new thought!

"I mean, that would explain it wouldn't it? Why he got in touch with you all after all these years?" She nodded. "I believe that the Holy Spirit is showing me that he *is* a Christian."

Danny knew he should be glad if that were true. But didn't that make it even more certain that God would want his parents to get married again?

As Danny turned to go, David said, "Wait a minute, Danny." Danny saw that the others were retrieving sacks from under that oil cloth.

They all said, at the same time, "Happy Birthday, Danny!" They each pulled out a gift for him. His birthday wasn't 'til Sunday but they said since most of them wouldn't see him then, they wanted to celebrate with him now.

Maggie set out a plate of chocolate chip cookies. "Your mom sent these. She knew about it." Maggie laughed. "We were glad you asked for a meeting because we were trying to figure out what excuse we would use to get you here."

~~~

Danny's father was supposed to arrive at 10 a.m. on Saturday morning and although Danny would have liked to stay asleep until about 15 minutes 'til 10, he set his alarm for 9 so he could eat breakfast and take a shower. But he awoke even earlier than usual ... at 6:30. He looked at the clock and groaned and rolled over, put the pillow over his head, and tried to go back to sleep.

But it was no use.

Danny grabbed his Bible from the bedside stand. He had decided to read the whole Bible and was now in the book of Deuteronomy. It was kind of boring most of the time but today a verse leaped out at him 33:27. *"The God who lives forever is your safe place. His arms are always under you. He drove away from in front of you those who hate you, and said 'Destroy!'"*

Danny lay the Bible face down on his stomach and closed his eyes. "Lord, you *are* my safe place. Help me to feel your arms protecting me. This says you will drive away those who hate me. Who *does* hate me? I know the kids prayed for me but I'm still scared. Unless you help me, I can't act right when he comes."

Danny was glad that Mom took off work today so she could be there with them. He knew he couldn't see his father alone. But then he wished that his father wouldn't see his mom at all. Danny put the Bible back on the table and curled back up in the blanket.

He reminded himself that underneath him were the everlasting arms. The next thing he knew was when the alarm rang.

It was one minute before ten when the knock came on the door. Danny's stomach felt like it had knots in it as well as a chunk of ice.

Mom opened the door and let *him* in. He had on a business suit. The dark thick eyebrows were just like Danny remembered.

His father and Mom looked at each other and then at the same time moved toward each other and hugged.

Danny wanted to hit the man and push him out the door. But within seconds his father turned toward Danny.

"Son," he said gently, waiting.

"Hello, Sir."

"Come on in and have a cup of coffee," Mom pointed the way to the kitchen.

When they were all seated around the table, his father said, "Oh, I almost forgot." He reached into the inside pocket of his jacket. "I told the attorney I would just bring this in person." He handed the envelope to Mom and they were all silent while she opened it and read the letter inside.

Danny saw that tears sprang to her eyes, and she pulled out a check from the envelope.

"I think that's right," his father said. He seemed nervous now. "The back payments for child support. I'll start paying them regularly now, starting next month. That should include this month. Is that right?"

Mom nodded and tears streamed down her cheeks. "Thank you," she said.

His father shook his head. "No! Thank YOU! This is so long overdue. I should have done something years ago. Well, I was embarrassed and then I wasn't sure how to find you and it was just easier to let it go … for a coward! Also, the last year I have been saving money to catch it all up."

He looked at Danny then. "I quit drinking about two years after I left you all but I didn't hand my life over to the Lord until last year." He turned back to Mom. "I know you prayed for me, that I'd become a Christian. Thank you for that too."

Mom just nodded her head but then her face crumpled and she started crying harder. Finally, she excused herself and went to the bathroom for tissues.

Danny's stomach knotted even tighter. He was now sure that God would want to put their family back together. His father seemed like a nice man, but did he really think he could come in here and buy them back?

"Son." His father was looking at him with love and sadness in his eyes.

Danny didn't want to look at him, but the love seemed to act as a magnet to his own eyes.

"Son, can you forgive me?"

Forgive? What does that mean? I don't want you to go to hell. But does forgive mean I have to belong to you? Have to do what you want? Does forgive mean I have to trust you?

"Son, I don't expect you to trust me, not right away. I hurt you and your mom over and over, first by mistreating you when I was here and then by neglecting you when I left. Your mother is a saint and I know you must really hate what I did to her, even more than what I did to you. But I guess what I am asking is if we could make a new start."

Danny's stomach not only clutched itself but he could feel burning in his throat. The thought came to him that this was what the commercials on TV were talking about when they said acid reflux. *How random!*

His father went on talking like he didn't know Danny was about to throw up.

"Son, I don't want to intrude on your life. I know you and your mom are happy. She tells me that she now has a man friend that you get along with very well."

Danny looked up. If Mom told him about Coach, maybe it wasn't as bad as it seemed.

"I don't want to intrude but I thought maybe we could start visiting. I'd like you to come to Texas and visit me for a week or two this summer. But I wouldn't ask that until I've come here some and we get to know each other better."

Danny could breathe now. He thought about it. *Okay, God. You're in charge here. I'm going to trust You, not him but you.*

He looked at his dad straight in the eyes. "Okay."

Joy sprang into the strange man's eyes right under the familiar eyebrows.

Just then Mom came back into the room.

She looked not at Danny but at his father. "Okay?"

"I think so." He turned to Danny. "Okay?"

Danny forced the corners of his mouth up. "Okay."

"Now, I have something else to tell you. Your mom knows this but we decided that I should tell you in person."

Danny waited. *What now?*

"I'd like for you two to go to lunch with me. I want you to meet someone." Danny's father looked nervous. "I'd like for you to meet your brother."

Danny's mouth flew open. *Brother?*

"My wife and son – other son – are at the motel now. We got

here last night. They really want to meet you … both of you."

A hot wave of relief flooded through Danny's body, melted the ice in his stomach, and soothed away the clenched muscles. He could feel a grin spreading across his face, and his cheeks almost hurt with the strength of the grin.

"You're married?"

Both his parents looked puzzled.

"Yes. Why does that make you so happy?" The curiosity was obvious in his father's voice.

Suddenly Mom smiled too and went over to stand behind Danny and lean down to give him a hug. "I think, and you can tell me if I'm wrong, I think Danny was afraid that maybe we might get back together. That would mean changes that Danny doesn't want. Is that right, Danny?" She turned Danny around to face her.

He could feel his cheeks turn red. He nodded.

"Well, I think I can promise you that neither your mom nor I want those changes either." His dad chuckled.

Then they all laughed together. It felt good.

≈≈≈

The next morning in church, Danny sat beside his brother, his new brother Alan who was six years old. Alan was on his right and Mom was on his left. On the other side of Mom was Coach Adams and on the other side of Alan was his dad. Beside his dad was Danny's stepmother, Jill, who was a really nice lady.

Danny thought about the meeting of the Fun To Be One Club two days ago and especially the prayers of Scooter and Gretchen, that God would surprise him with fun with his father, and Ray's prayer that Danny would see the good in his father.

Danny thought about the lunch with his mom and the others when he met Alan and Jill. He thought about the afternoon yesterday playing miniature golf with his new family, his dad, and his brother, and his stepmother. Fun and surprises … and seeing good in someone he had always thought had no good in him. In seeing that good, something in Danny left, something bad, something that was ashamed of who he was because of who his father was.

It was Danny's birthday, the best birthday he ever had.

But it was also Easter Sunday, Resurrection Day, the new beginning for the world.

The congregation sang, and Danny sang out with great joy.

The day of resurrection! Earth, tell it out abroad;
the passover of gladness, the passover of God.
From death to life eternal, from earth unto the sky,
our Christ hath brought us over, with hymns of victory.

Victory. Danny remembered the scripture verse that God spoke to him yesterday morning. *"The God who lives forever is your safe place. His arms are always under you. He drove away from in front of you those who hate you, and said 'Destroy!'"*

Danny had wondered who hated him – who his enemies were. Now he knew. Danny's only enemy, the only enemy of all people was the father of lies, the source of fear. God had thrust him out of Danny's mind and his heart.

With the help of God and the Fun To Be One Club, and the Church, and his family ... and at that thought Danny looked past his mom over at Coach Adams who just happened to be looking at Danny and who winked ... Danny would make sure that those lies and fears were destroyed.

They started singing one of Danny's favorite songs. A great song for Easter, about Jesus being alive and making life worthwhile for others.

It wasn't bad to be Danny Alcorn any more.

A brand new life stretched ahead of him. The FUN TO BE ONE CLUB Camp, a visit to Texas, Mom being able to quit her second job. And Coach ... Mom even said they could visit the church where David and Coach went, some Sunday night soon.

Danny's life was definitely worth living now, because Jesus is alive!

Which Witch? Discussions for Friends and Family

1) Danny is a new kid in school. How does that make people feel? Have you ever gone to a new place where everyone else knows each other? If you have, was it scary? What could you do to make new kids feel more welcome in your school? Neighborhood? Church?

2) Have you ever been bullied by another kid? Have you ever been a bully – or been tempted to be one? What should a kid do if they are being bullied?

3) Do you think witchcraft is real? What did you find out about it in this book?

4) Did you see anything in the book that makes you think these words in I Corinthians 13:8 "Love never fails." are true? If so how many things did you see?

5) The kids in this book go to many different kinds of churches. Do you think there is just one church that is right about everything or do you think that all churches have some truth in them?

6) Who were your favorite characters in the book? Which boy? Which girl? Which adult? Why are they your favorites?

7) Which characters in the book did you dislike? Why?

8) Did you learn anything about the difference in just believing in the history about Jesus and knowing Him personally? Do you want to know Him better? Do you believe you can?

9) Would you like to have a Fun To Be One Club in your community? What could you do to help start one?

10) Would you like to belong to an online Fun To Be One Club? You can join at www.FTBOclub.com. It's free, and your e–mail address will never be given to anyone else.

Hey Kids,

Come Join the

Fun To Be One

Club

It's Free! It's Fun!

 www.FTBOclub.com

To Parents of young readers,

I'm glad you are checking this page out. I am very protective of the minds of all children. There is nothing in this book that I have not seen or experienced myself. As you and your child will find out, all is not always as it appears. In these days we live in, where evil abounds in everything from bullies to the supernatural, it's important for Christian young people to understand their relationship and place of authority in Christ Jesus. This book and its sequels are my attempt to help equip them.

The last names of the children who first read and commented on the book are withheld in order to protect them. I pray for you and your children, that you may be blessed, encouraged, and empowered by the Holy Spirit through the books in the Fun To Be One Club series.

Sincerely,

Amy Barkman

About Amy Barkman

I was sprinkled as a young child and raised Presbyterian, led to accept Jesus by a nun in a Catholic school, became a Sunday School teacher and youth group leader in a Reformation Christian Church where I was immersed. I was an elder in a non–denominational church and during moves to other towns and states I became a member of a Baptist Church, a Congregational Church, a home church, and am now a Methodist. Some of my best friends are Episcopalian, Pentecostal, Lutheran, and Church of God.

I am the Director of Voice of Joy Ministries, which is trans–denominational and sponsors the Fun To Be One Club. I'm part of the Unity in the Community pastor's group in my hometown. I have a passion for Jesus and unity in His Body. I am happily married to Gary Barkman. Between us we have seven children, thirteen grandchildren, and one great–grandchild.

Visit Amy on the Web:

www.AmyBarkman.com